HIDDEN AFFECTION

Marianne watched the children troop out with a mixture of relief and chagrin. She did not know quite how to characterize what had just passed, nor what to expect from the doctor. Perhaps he would not let them come again. She would miss them.

"You did not tell me you were a miracle worker," the doctor said quietly when they were left alone.

She stole a glance at him, and was relieved to see the ghost of a smile tracing his lips. "I do not believe I have seen Charlie and George so still," he said, "and they were not asleep. And was that little Becky's voice I heard as I came in?"

So he had been there that long. She nodded, unsure how to respond. The silence that interposed was past bearing. "I am sorry, doctor. I did not mean to say such things. That is, I did, but . . ."

"Mrs. Glencoe, Mrs. Glencoe," he whispered. Then he took her hand in his and, raising it to his lips, kissed it as if it were the dearest thing on earth.

ZEBRA'S REGENCY ROMANCES
DAZZLE AND DELIGHT

A BEGUILING INTRIGUE (4441, $3.99)
by Olivia Sumner

Pretty as a picture Justine Riggs cared nothing for propriety. She dressed as a boy, sat on her horse like a jockey, and pondered the stars like a scientist. But when she tried to best the handsome Quenton Fletcher, Marquess of Devon, by proving that she was the better equestrian, he would try to prove Justine's antics were pure folly. The game he had in mind was seduction—never imagining that he might lose his heart in the process!

AN INCONVENIENT ENGAGEMENT (4442, $3.99)
by Joy Reed

Rebecca Wentworth was furious when she saw her betrothed waltzing with another. So she decides to make him jealous by flirting with the handsomest man at the ball, John Collinwood, Earl of Stanford. The "wicked" nobleman knew exactly what the enticing miss was up to—and he was only too happy to play along. But as Rebecca gazed into his magnificent eyes, her errant fiancé was soon utterly forgotten!

SCANDAL'S LADY (4472, $3.99)
by Mary Kingsley

Cassandra was shocked to learn that the new Earl of Lynton was her childhood friend, Nicholas St. John. After years at sea and mixed feelings Nicholas had come home to take the family title. And although Cassandra knew her place as a governess, she could not help the thrill that went through her each time he was near. Nicholas was pleased to find that his old friend Cassandra was his new next door neighbor, but after being near her, he wondered if mere friendship would be enough . . .

HIS LORDSHIP'S REWARD (4473, $3.99)
by Carola Dunn

As the daughter of a seasoned soldier, Fanny Ingram was accustomed to the vagaries of military life and cared not a whit about matters of rank and social standing. So she certainly never foresaw her *tendre* for handsome Viscount Roworth of Kent with whom she was forced to share lodgings, while he carried out his clandestine activities on behalf of the British Army. And though good sense told Roworth to keep his distance, he couldn't stop from taking Fanny in his arms for a kiss that made all hearts equal!

Fortune's Mistress
Mary Chase Comstock

ZEBRA BOOKS
KENSINGTON PUBLISHING CORP.

ZEBRA BOOKS are published by

Kensington Publishing Corp.
850 Third Avenue
New York, NY 10022

First Printing: February, 1996
10 9 8 7 6 5 4 3 2 1

Printed in the United States of America

One

Sir Frederick Stratford reclined lazily on a settee before a window which opened onto a small decorative garden. The bright morning sunlight framed his head, making it difficult for Marianne to judge his expression. She could guess, however. She had sometimes reflected, when she gave him any thought at all, that Stratford seemed to have made the cultivation of ironic weariness his life's study. When he smiled, however (and this was a rare occurrence), he reminded her of a cat toying with a mouse in its claws.

No, she did not like Sir Frederick. His unblinking stare made her apprehensive in a way she did not wish to examine; she rarely denied him her presence when he happened to call, however. Who, after all, was she, to deny her presence to anyone?

"And so, my dear Marianne," he drawled, "you must tell me. Dare I cherish a hope that our young friend, Cheswick, has at last grown tired of your charms?"

With an effort, Marianne fought back a disagreeable shudder at the insinuation his words conveyed. Instead, she smiled sweetly. "Why ever do you ask, Sir Frederick? Do I look hagged this morning?"

She knew quite well she did not—although she had every reason to do so on this lovely late spring morning. She had dressed herself with her habitual care in a rose-colored gown. Her sable hair was elegantly coiled, and accented by a spray of new roses. Her studied demeanor, she knew, projected a calm equal to that of the fine weather of June.

"Of course not, my dear. You know it as well as I, and I wish you will not play such games with me. You look as you have looked these past five years: like a pale pearlescent seashell, I have often thought." He took a pinch of snuff, applied it, and sneezed delicately into his handkerchief. "No," he went on, "we both know I ask merely out of self-interest. If you were, for the nonce, without a sponsor, it would be a sorry thing indeed were I to let pass such an opportune moment simply by virtue of your stoicism. Tell me, do you never weep or rail when your gentlemen leave you?"

"Weep?" she returned with a laugh of dismay. "What a notion! Why ever should I weep?"

"Come, now," he chided, looking at her narrowly through his eyepiece. "Have you not loved any of them then? Not even a little?"

She covered the silent moment which ensued by taking the last sip from her teacup and returning it calmly to its saucer. Why, after all, should she divulge her secrets to anyone? She had found to her sorrow that there was nothing to gain by sharing confidences.

She looked up at him. "More tea, Sir Frederick?"

He shook his head impatiently. "Do not avoid my question."

She poured for herself, then shrugged as she settled back into her chair. "If I do so, it is because your question has not a good answer."

"Not a *witty* answer, you mean." He leaned forward. Now she could see the gleam in his otherwise lazy, downturned eyes. "And that is why *I* suspect that *you* suspect Cheswick will soon bid his fond *adieux*. I have observed you are far too careful of your beauty to allow the shadow of misfortune to dull it. But the razor of your repartee?" He shook his head. "That is an altogether different question, my dear."

"You are boring this morning, Sir Frederick," she told him plainly. "It is not to be wondered at if I cannot summon a spark of conversation, when there is none to which I can respond."

"Little witch!" he laughed. "So you still have some barbs to cast my way!"

"Of course," she replied pleasantly. "I saved them especially for you. You know quite well I cannot bear to see you disappointed."

"Aha!" he said, leaning more closely toward her. "Dare I hope you might harbor some small tenderness for me, if for no one else?"

She took a sip of tea before replying. "No, you dare not. I merely mean that when all does not go exactly as you please, your lugubrious expression quite sets my teeth on edge."

He stood slowly and moved beside her chair, placing his hands on her shoulders. The gesture was unsettling, and with an effort, she fought back the thin shiver it sent up her spine.

"Come now. Would it be so very bad, my dear?" he murmured, tracing the line of her neck with a fingertip. "We have known each other this age— we are, both of us, cold realists. I should think we would rub on quite comfortably together."

She gave a short laugh, pulling away from his touch. "I shudder to think what your notion of comfortable must be, Sir Frederick." She rose and walked to the window, then turned to face him. "It is no secret you have not two guineas to rub together."

His eyes narrowed for a second at this affront, before he went on smoothly, "How unkind you are, Marianne— for all it is one of your most charming traits— but I must tell you, I have done exceedingly well at the tables these last weeks."

She cocked her head and studied him for a moment. "Ah, I begin to see. I collect you are now in possession of four guineas?"

"I have considerably more than that at my disposal!" he said, his tone growing sharp. "Believe me, I could take care of your needs well enough."

"For the present, that may be so," she allowed, "but for how much longer? Remember, my dear Sir Frederick, you cannot pawn *me* as if I were a family heirloom."

"What a blatant little materialist you are!" he snapped, coloring. He turned and paced impatiently for a moment. "Must you always weigh a man's purse as if it were his very soul?"

Marianne took pains to school her expression. Sir Frederick was never one to honey his observations with euphemisms. It would never do to show him just how much, how deeply his words cut.

"How unfortunate that I must do so." She gestured at the stylishly appointed salon. "Let us be plain. We speak, after all, of my livelihood. How can you expect anything else?"

"It is your extraordinarily sweet face that accounts for my folly," he said, perusing her thoughtfully for a moment. Then he made her a stiff bow. "I sometimes forget that the shriveled heart of a shopkeeper lies behind its lovely facade."

As he picked up his walking stick and gloves, he added softly, "Do not forget, however, that you have made yourself merchandise— and that I should like very much to see that silky hair uncoiled about your shoulders. Trust me, my dear, I shall some day. I need merely to find your price. Good day, Marianne."

Later, as she supervised the packing of her trunks in her chamber, Marianne stopped for a moment and petulantly considered her reflection in the mirror. Her face was a pale oval, framed by her glossy dark hair. Her eyes, a clear hyacinth, were fringed with dark luxuriant lashes. Her figure was still lithe. But Sir Frederick was right. Her exterior bore no clue to what she had become on the inside. The heart of a shopkeeper, he had said.

What other choice did he think she had? she wondered angrily. What choice, for that matter, did any woman have? It was no secret that the hallowed halls of Almack's were as much a marketplace for human flesh and fortune as any Haymarket street corner. But for the heart of a shopkeeper, that might have been her fate as well. Had she not schemed and calculated, had she not accepted *carte blanche* from protectors, she might very well have been forced to recourse to the streets.

Without the heart of a shopkeeper, her choices would have been nonexistent. They were few enough as it was. One foolish moment had banished the meager freedoms allowed a woman.

The image of the season on which she had embarked all those years ago rose up before her, and Marianne experienced a sharp familiar pang. The veiled pandering, the false fronts of the *ton*. Her younger self decked out in costumes of virginal white, her mind full of romantic notions. What foolishness it had all been! She quickly banished that picture to the recesses of her heart, pulling a veil over the scene with a practiced hand.

Stratford was quite correct in his assessment that she was now without a sponsor, but he was several weeks behind in this realization. Monte

Cheswick had made his departure some time ago, in the face of his engagement to a young lady whose parents were as high sticklers as they were wealthy. They would not countenance, he had told Marianne, his association with her, and had insisted it be broken off before the papers were drawn up.

"I do not at all like to leave you, Marianne, for you must know I have grown quite fond of you. What's more, I welcome the notion of being leg-shackled to Miss Carruthers as much as I might an invitation to a fusty musical evening! A tedious companion she'll be, I can tell you— though her father is rich as a pudding— and monstrous plate-faced into the bargain. There is nothing I can do, however. My parents— they are altogether Old Testament, you know!— would have it so. We younger sons must ever be sacrificed to family consequence.

"This," he went on gruffly, handing her a velvet box, "is purchased with the last of my *own* blunt."

She opened it slowly and held back a gasp. A great many diamonds set in gold sparkled back at her. "Are you certain? It is not," she asked in some alarm, "a family piece?"

"No," he admitted, "though I should not grudge it you. I particularly wanted you to have something to remember me by."

Ironic, she had thought, that he should have chosen those particular words. Soon enough, she would have a memento of him, an all too tangible one.

When he had left a short time later, bidding her good fortune, she had stood a while, letting the diamonds of the choker sift through her fingers like crystaline drops of water. It would cost her to part with them. Jeweled tributes she had received from other gentlemen had rarely been in such good taste, but for all his youth, Cheswick had a better understanding of her and her sensibilities than any of his predecessors.

She did not for a moment contemplate keeping the necklace, however. Considering her present situation, it would be the height of foolishness. She could not, now, allow herself to be self-indulgent. Besides, she had told herself, there would never again be the least occasion for wearing such a piece. For the foreseeable future, she must deck herself in black sarsenet; her only adornment must be a simple onyx mourning brooch. Therein rested hope.

Perhaps it was bred of stubbornness, but, through the years, Marianne had never allowed herself to forsake the belief that some day, somehow, the path to a brighter future must open before her. She would not permit the despair she sometimes felt to overtake her, for in that avenue, she knew, lay madness.

At first, when she was younger, she had thought that love might still find a way. She dreamed that some good man, for she knew they existed, would overlook her past and take her away from all her folly had ordained.

As the years passed, however, she realized that

if she were to be rescued, it must be through her own ingenuity. She had begun saving for the future, therefore, ignoring the wounds to her pride as she accepted more and more gifts from those whose patronage she endured. She had sold jewelry, gifts, economized her house-keeping, until she had at last accumulated a considerable amount. Until the realization that she was with child, she had planned to merely retire altogether from the life she knew. But now she had reason beyond her own salvation to do so, a joyous reason which must quickly be addressed.

"There's a gentleman to see you downstairs in the bookroom, ma'am."

Brought back to the present, Marianne glanced at the card the maidservant handed her. "Tell Mr. Needham I shall be down in a moment."

There was no need to tidy her hair, but she patted it, nonetheless, out of habit. She did not wish to present herself to the caller too quickly, or appear too eager. No, she must let him wait at least ten minutes. Perhaps more. She lingered some time, therefore, instructing the servants as to which items she wished to bring with her to the countryside. Later, she would assemble and pack a mourning wardrobe on her own. Her staff knew quite well what she was, but she did not wish them to know her plans any more than was necessary, nor to raise questions she would not like to answer.

She made her tardy appearance some twenty minutes after Mr. Needham arrived. As she quietly entered the bookroom, she caught him examining the potter's mark on a Chinese vase, his bent figure resembling a scrawled question mark. He set the vase down quickly at her greeting, and turned his posture to a slightly deeper bow.

"Good morning, Miss Gardiner." A smile eased slowly across his face as if he were unaccustomed to such an undertaking. "I trust I have not waited upon you too early."

"Indeed not," she told him as she seated herself at the desk. "I believe I requested you call as soon as you had arrived at a figure."

His smile vanished more quickly than it had appeared, and he immediately assumed a more businesslike demeanor. "The diamonds are quite fine," he told her. "Quite the best specimens you have offered."

She knew this very well, and acknowledged his appraisal with a questioning lift of her eyebrows.

"I can make you a price of £500 now," he told her, "but there are several regular buyers whom I expect to see this month. If one of them were to make an offer, I might be able to do even better."

She nodded, calculating silently how much longer she dared stay in London. Sir Frederick's call this morning had unnerved her. It was well, she reflected, that all was in readiness for her departure. She might even depart next week, if she so chose. The sooner she left, the better.

Last week she had finalized the purchase of

a small house in Cornwall, not far from Land's
End. She knew little of the district other than
its remoteness and a few childhood tales of
hauntings and enchantments, but the notion of
leaving the city at last for a place known as the
end of the earth appealed to her overwhelm-
ingly.

Still, the difference a hundred or more
pounds might make was not insignificant. Behind the desk, she placed a tentative hand above
her gradually increasing womb. Before long, she
would be unable to hide her condition, and she
wanted no suspicion of the reason for her quitting London to be bandied about.

"I believe I will accept the figure you suggest," she said quietly.

Mr. Needham nodded without further comment and pulled a bank draft from his satchel.
He signed it over to her with a flourish.

"As always, it is a pleasure to do business with
you, Miss Gardiner. You are quite a . . . practical woman."

He departed soon after, leaving Marianne to
ponder the draft he had left on the table. The
£500 would cushion the next several years considerably. She was certain she could engage a
nurse for her child now, and tutors or a governess when the time came. Whatever the cost to
her pride during such calls as had just passed,
the welfare of her child, the opportunity to leave
her sordid past behind and assume a new life,
must be ensured.

Now that her business with Needham had

been concluded, there was little to keep her in town. Everything was in readiness, her carefully drawn plans realized. She was taking little with her besides clothing, books, and a few keepsakes. In spite of the fine spring weather, she felt she could not endure London another day.

And there was but one more appointment to keep, one farewell which must be made.

Two

A scarce hour later, Marianne sat on a bench beneath a grove of trees in Hyde Park, waiting. It was quiet, not yet the fashionable hour for driving out, so she was quite safe from the sharp glances of curious eyes. Still, she had maintained an exceedingly private life, and it always made her nervous to expose herself thus. In spite of the passage of time, she knew quite well her name was still noised about. The mere mention of the name Marianne Gardiner was used as an admonition to heedless young ladies, whose high-spirited behavior had alerted their watchful mamas to the disaster to which their hoydenish tendencies might lead. Her name was synonymous with the spectre of such a disgraceful future.

A slight breeze prompted a shiver in spite of the clear spring sunlight, and Marianne wished she had worn a spencer instead of a shawl. Poets might celebrate the beauties of early June, but she was certain they must have found their inspiration while well wrapped against the changeable weather.

As was her custom at these meetings, she had

changed from her rose morning gown to an un-remarkable walking dress of a dullish hue. It was best for all concerned that none should have cause to note her presence.

At precisely three o'clock, a familiar carriage slowed along the drive and a lady, followed by her maid, alit. Marianne watched as the driver was told to return in an hour's time. Just as she did each month, the maid crossed the green to another bench where she sat and took out some needlework. The lady made her way to Mari-anne's side and, without ceremony, held out her hands to her.

"You are quite lovely this afternoon, Olivia," Marianne said as she kissed the other's cheek. Her remark was not a mere pleasantry. Olivia shared Marianne's flawless complexion and, though her hair was a rich chestnut, her eyes flashed the same startling hyacinth blue. Ironi-cally, fortune had allowed her elder sister to re-tain the lightness of expression so often reserved only for happy childhood years, and she was, indeed, beautiful.

Marianne patted the seat beside her. "Are Mama and Papa well?" she asked with forced brightness.

Olivia sighed as she seated herself. "They are, of course, but are most careful not to admit it. Mama spends most of the day lamenting her treacherous nerves, while Papa makes a lively discussion of his gout, but you needn't unsettle yourself. I suspect these are merely symptoms of boredom and self-absorption."

Marianne nodded. 'Twas ever thus with them. She harbored no affection for her parents, but she knew her sister did so out of an unquestioning sense of duty. As Olivia prattled on about their various complaints and eccentricities, Marianne swallowed back the bleak emotions which swirled at the thought of her father and mother. Olivia's complacency was understandable. Owing to the fact that she was enjoying an extended wedding trip at the time of Marianne's entry into society, Olivia had never known the whole of her parents' response to the scandal—the beatings, the recriminations they had rained down upon Marianne when they had learned of her folly.

By the time the new Lady Blakensly returned, her younger sister had already embarked on the life of a demirep, the life she had been forced to choose. Despite Olivia's tearful pleadings, Marianne had refused to accept her sister's offer of a refuge in her own home, and the episode remained something the sisters did not discuss.

"And William and the children?" Marianne continued, turning the conversation. "How do they fare?"

At the mention of her family, Olivia's expression became more animated. "Dear little Maria cut her first tooth this week, and has already contrived to bite Nurse with it!"

"Charmer!" Marianne laughed.

"And young Justin has made the acquaintance of his first tutor. I cannot but fear the gentleman is too strict with him, although William merely smiles at my apprehensions, and assures me a bit of discipline is good for him." She shook her head. "My husband insists— in the nicest way possible, you know— I have indulged the lad shockingly, but I cannot agree. I simply like to see my children happy."

"And how does your William get on?" Marianne had never met her sister's husband, but was grateful to him nonetheless for countenancing these precious meetings. Few others would have been so liberal-minded.

"Very well indeed." Olivia's face lit with clear affection and pride. When a cloud of scandal had overhung the family so soon after his entry to it, he had helped Olivia to brave it out, using his name and influence to compel the *ton's* acceptance of his new wife. "He will assume his seat when next the House meets. He says it is a mere nothing, but I know he is as delighted as I. I only hope he will not object, if I wish to attend the first session."

"Why ever should he object?" Marianne asked. "I should think he would wish your presence above all things, my sweet, he is so besotted with you."

Olivia blushed and took her younger sister's hand. "You see, the session will not be for some little time and . . . I am once more *enceinte.*"

"You are . . . with child?" Marianne asked, her voice wavering. Although she could never begrudge her sister any joy, she felt her throat tighten painfully. How different would be the upbringing of Olivia's child, and the one she herself now carried. One fêted and fussed over by all and sundry. The other reared in a cloud of seclusion, however loving.

"Is it not splendid!" Olivia threw back her head and hugged herself. "I had hoped, of course, but I did not dream it would be so soon. There is nothing in the world so joyous as a tiny new baby, Marianne. How I wish you could know what it is— "

She stopped herself suddenly, looking abashed. "You must forgive me, dearest. How foolish of me to run on so, when my enthusing must surely give you nothing but pain. I know you never like to speak of yourself, but it always seems as if I never allow my tongue a rest, even should you wish to be more forthcoming."

"Do not worry," Marianne said softly. She looked down for a moment at her gloved hands before going on. "I should never have survived these last years, had I not known I would see you here each month and hear about— "

She stopped herself short of saying the words that were on her tongue: *Hear about the life I might have had*. Still, she herself was about to embark on a new life. The shadow of regret which had hung over her so long must be banished for good and all. There was reason for celebration on both their parts, if only Olivia would see it that way. "However, I shall surprise you today, Olivia. There *is* something important I must tell you."

A flicker of concern darkened Olivia's blue eyes.

"There now, it is not so very dreadful," her sister assured her. "In fact, on the whole, it is something very good indeed."

Olivia looked doubtful, her question showing clearly in her eyes: how could anything under the sun improve her sister's lot? Then her expression brightened and she jumped to her feet, clapping her hands together in joyful surprise. "What a great dolt I am not to have thought of it at once! It is Monte Cheswick, is it not? He has asked you to marry him!"

Marianne quickly negated that possibility with a shake of her head. "What? Do you think I should allow myself to ruin yet another life? I hope I have not given you reason to think of such a thing, Olivia. I would not stoop to such a trick as to accept him, even were he so foolish as to ask." She took a deep breath before going on. "The truth is, I shall be leaving London. Next week, in fact, if all goes as I plan."

Olivia gasped and whirled toward her. "Leaving London?!"

"Yes. No one must know, but I shall soon be quitting the city for good, departing for the country. Alone."

"Departing . . . ?" Olivia stared at her blankly. "But what does this mean? How? Where? And for heaven's sake, *why?*"

"I can supply the answers to your questions far more easily than I arrived at them, I can tell you," she returned, holding out her hand once more. Olivia took it in her own, but Marianne could feel a tremor run between them. "Calm yourself, dear. All it really means is that I shall at last have some independence. As to how, I have had for some time an amount put by for the occasion. Where . . . I am afraid it must be Cornwall. I require a remote location."

"Remote! Cornwall!" Olivia pulled away from her. "You might as well have said Australia! For God's sake, Marianne, tell me, why must you go so far?"

Marianne leaned her head back and stared up into the spacious blue above her for a long moment, avoiding her sister's piercing eye. "It is merely, my dear," she said at last, "that, like you, I am with child."

Olivia sank to the bench beside her, entirely still for a moment, silent for once. The breeze ruffled the newly leafed trees, but no other sound intruded. Silhouetted against the bright sky, Olivia's profile revealed the set of a strong-willed chin. She looked for all the world as she had when they were both children, and some nursery battle was about to be engaged. At last, she stood and attempted a thin smile.

"Let us walk a little, Marianne," she said. Although she maintained her demeanor admirably, Olivia's voice faltered, weak as a girl's. "Of a sudden, my head feels as if it has been rolled up in cobwebs. I fear it must be cleared, before I can comprehend this business."

Marianne arose, and the sisters made their way down a secluded walk. Still silent, she noted abstractedly that the earlier blossoms of spring had faded into little piles of withered gold and purple, like miniature gowns discarded after a ball. How many centuries had it been since she and Olivia had daydreamed about the revels of fairy folk, dancing till first light in spring gardens? In spite of the new life within her, she felt very old indeed.

"What does Cheswick say to this?" Olivia broke into her thoughts.

"Cheswick . . ." Marianne began, then hesitated. She knew quite well what her sister's response would be, and steeled herself for it. "I am afraid Cheswick . . . does not know."

"Does not know!" Olivia choked. "Why did you not tell him at once?"

"To what end?" she asked simply.

"To what end!" Olivia's eyes flashed. "Only consider your situation. You are alone, without protection or support. How can you be so idiotic?"

"Listen but a moment," Marianne said calmly. "I know I must seem foolish— "

"*Seem!*"

"— but trust me. I do know what I am about. To begin with, Cheswick is about to be married."

"All the more reason he should know!" Olivia insisted. "It is no secret his will be nothing more than an alliance of estates. If only he knew, he might— "

"I know. He might feel duty bound to make some settlement on me, true, but I am not . . . the sort of woman for whom sacrifices are made. Nor do I wish to be. In any case," she went on quickly, "I shall get along quite nicely without his support. I have already purchased a small house. I have enough put aside to provide for myself and the babe for the foreseeable future."

"So you will go to the end of the earth?" her sister said bleakly. "You cannot know about childbirth, Marianne. It is no easy thing, for all I have been so fortunate. And in Cornwall! You will be hard-pressed to find an apothecary to attend you, let alone a surgeon."

"Country women have been bearing children for centuries, Olivia," she said wryly, "and seemingly with less difficulty than is met in the city, for all our learned physicians."

"Are you absolutely determined in this course?"

Marianne nodded.

"Then we shall never meet again," her sister said hopelessly.

"Of course, we shall. It will simply be more difficult to arrange." She walked ahead a bit, frowning. Leaving Olivia, indeed, was her only regret. She would see her sister again, though. She would make sure. "Olivia," she said softly, as she turned and stretched out her hand. "Will you not see that this is the only way? Will you not wish me happy?"

Tears sparkled in Olivia's eyes, and she could feel them rising in her own. "How can you doubt me?" her sister asked, her voice trembling. "I have ever wished, prayed, that some happiness might be yours. I have been so blessed in life! It has hurt me to my core to see you so isolated, so chained to a fate that, through a moment's folly, might have been anyone's."

Marianne shook her head. "I was altogether foolish."

"You were trusting," Olivia exclaimed bitterly. "Were we not raised to be biddable and sweet? To yield to whatever whims— "

"Do you not see?" Marianne interrupted. "It simply does not matter anymore. It is time to forget the past. And now— now I have the ability, the opportunity, indeed, the duty to do so. To leave it behind, and start two new lives." She paused and blinked back the tears. "Perhaps," she went on, "that way I can still make something good from all of this."

Olivia pulled her shawl more tightly about her and looked up into the sky. "You will have all my thoughts and prayers," she whispered.

"And your silence?" Marianne asked. "No one must know of this."

Her sister attempted a smile. "Except for William. He does ask after you, you know, although you have never met. And I keep no secrets from my husband."

Marianne nodded silently, as she wondered for the hundredth time what it would be to enjoy such a companionship. She did not know what the future held, but she prayed that a measure of happiness would not be forever withheld.

Three

Marianne sat back on her knees and wiped her hands on her apron, before bracing them against the dull ache in her back. How good it was to be in a garden, to be nurturing green things! She had never before been allowed the freedom to plunge her hands into soil, and she did so these days with enthusiasm. The smell of the earth was sweet, and her heart was light.

Even though she had been engaged in her new life less than two months, she surveyed the scene before her with satisfaction: a garden of her very own. Despite the waning summer, the flower beds were wild with color, pink clashing against gold against violet, like a disheveled trunk of bright silk ball gowns.

That was what she liked best about the garden, she decided. Years of neglect had allowed it its own beauty. Grown beyond artificial borders, it was no longer forced into any shape except that which nature intended. All evidence of patterned pathways lined with stiff rows had been erased, and she planted and pruned judiciously, respecting the wildness which held sway here. Now opening as the sunlight arched above the rooftop, the flowers looked carelessly lovely, as if they had just arisen.

In a way, this late summer blossoming mirrored her own state, she thought with a slight smile. It was just as well, however, that summer would soon be coming to an end. Already, the sun seemed paler in the sky than it had a month ago. Soon enough she would be unequal to such exertion as had been her custom these last weeks. A winter fireside and a pile of novels would hold a charm of their own, she was sure.

Marianne looked fondly toward her house. Rosewood Cottage was as sweet a haven as she could have dreamt. Its rosy bricks were partially obscured by ivy, and the diamond pane windows glinted as they caught the sun. It was all her own, hers and the babe's.

She had stepped with very little difficulty from her old life into the new. But what difficulty could there be, she asked herself, moving from the constraints imposed by censure to the freedom of anonymity? From being a possession, to again commanding her own destiny? Erasing a sordid past and replacing it with innocent new life?

Despite her fears, no one in the village seemed to question the arrival of the "newly widowed" mother-to-be. Her story of a husband killed on the Peninsula was not unusual. Nor did she deny the rumor that had somehow arisen that his top-lofty family had turned their collective back on her. For the most part, the villagers seemed content to leave her to the solitude of widowhood, and happy enough that her purchase and tenancy of the cottage would generate positions for several of their sons and daughters.

She arose from her knees and stretched in the bright sunlight. Kneeling in the damp earth had made her a little stiff, and the notion of a ramble over the hills now seemed the very thing. She fetched a shawl from the house, for the wind off the sea seemed sometimes to penetrate to her very bones, then strolled off into the countryside.

A winding path led the way to a green dale she had grown fond of, where a circle of stones, centuries old, stood stark against the horizon. She had encountered few other people on previous walks, and none in the vicinity of the stone circle. Local legend told of seven virgins who had been turned to stone there for dancing on the Sabbath, and the country folk considered the place to be haunted by both the spirits of the poor damsels and the fairy folk with which the land, she was told, abounded. In a way, it seemed she haunted it herself, for since she had first discovered the circle and heard the stories, she had returned to it time and again.

Around the stones, she saw that bunches of bright violet flowers had sprung up since her last visit, and she stooped to pick a few. When she and Olivia had been children, it was their custom to fashion crowns for themselves out of any hapless wildflowers they discovered, and her fingers began to fashion a coronet, seemingly of their own accord.

Marianne seated herself on one of the stones which had fallen sideways in the grass, and looked out over the landscape which stretched forward, green and gold, before giving way to more rugged outcroppings of dark rock. In the far distance, the dull roar of the sea made its timeless complaint.

She had fashioned two small crowns when she heard an uneven gait approaching through the grass. Startled, she looked up and saw to her dismay a golden hound running toward her on three legs, its left quarter dipping as it bounded toward her. She sat perfectly still as the dog slowed, then ambled up and lay its large head in her lap, looking up at her with huge brown eyes. Her uncertainty faded.

"And where have you sprung from?" she asked as she began to stroke its head. "Did the fairy folk conjure you up to bear me company, or are you merely one of their number in disguise?"

The dog yawned, then cast his soulful eyes up to her, as if to say he would certainly tell her if only he could. He leaned heavily into her as she scratched under his chin, and she saw that, though the dog was missing a leg, the wound was long healed and had closed almost invisibly. Along the thin scar she thought she could perceive faint evidence of stitches having once been set there. Who would take such care, go to such expense for a dog? she wondered.

The dog sniffed at the flower wreaths that still lay in her lap, and, laughing, she placed one on

his golden head and, in a extravagant moment
of whimsy, another on her own. Panting, he
smiled up at her in a doggish grin.

"There," she said softly. "Though autumn is
on the air, we shall both be crowned with summer while we may."

Just then, the dog pricked up his ears and
turned away from her. Almost at once, she
heard a distant voice call, "Caliban! Where the
devil have you gone? Here, boy!"

The dog wheeled away from her at this sum-
mons, the crown falling down over one ear as
he ran. The sound of a human voice brought
Marianne to her feet. She spun from her perch
with an apprehensive start, and stepped behind
the nearest stone pillar.

Although she could not yet see the stranger,
Marianne immediately had recognized in his
tones the inflection of her own class. This was
no mere countryman, but one who had undeniably sprung from the heart of the *ton*. The
sensation of vulnerability, the fear of exposure,
washed over her like a sudden shower, prompting a shudder she was unable to quell. As she
flattened herself against the stone, she experienced as well an odd annoyance rising in her at
the notion of an intruder in her dale. She recognized quite well the foolishness of such a feeling, but still, she felt deflated, as if a magic spell
had been broken.

"Good boy, Caliban, but what is this?"

Marianne peeped out from her shelter behind
the stone column, and caught a glimpse of the

gentleman as he emerged and knelt beside the
dog. He fingered the wreath curiously for a moment before saying, "I cannot but say it becomes
you, friend."

He looked about, then caught sight of Marianne before she could slip behind the boulder
once more. He approached her at once, and
closer inspection of him brought Marianne up
short, for he was not at all what she had anticipated. His accent had brought to mind the polished figure and style of a Corinthian. She
expected hair à la Brutus, and a cravat done in
the Mathematical at the very least. The gentleman who greeted her just then fit this picture
not at all.

His hair was bright gold and badly in need
of cutting; his linen was tied in a simple knot.
While aristocratic, his face was marred by a long
fine scar, which traced a path from his chin to
his left ear. It looked, she thought unaccountably, as if he had been grazed by the sharp steel
edge of an angel's wing in some encounter between the celestial and the mundane.

There was something more, though. The gentleman looked . . . alive. That was the only word
for it. His eyes smiled, his color was high. When
he moved, it was with true purpose, rather than
mere achievement of effect. The impact of his
presence, of his eyes on her, was almost palpa-
ble, so very different from that of the indolent
rakes who had until recently comprised her male
acquaintance.

He stepped forward, smiling pleasantly, as he

placed one hand dramatically over his breast, " 'Most sure the goddess on whom these airs attend! Vouchsafe my prayer may know if you remain upon this island and that you will some good instruction give how I may bear me here; my prime request which I do last pronounce, is, O you wonder! if you be maid or no?' "

" 'No wonder, sir,' " Marianne replied, recognizing Shakespeare's lines from *The Tempest*, " 'but . . . ' " Her voice trailed off as she recalled the remainder of the speech, *but certainly a maid.* That would never do, for she had been anything but a maiden these five years. As the words died on her lips, she felt the color rise to her cheeks.

When the gentleman stood before her, he executed a deep bow and, despite her chagrin, Marianne felt a smile tug at the corners of her lips. It had been a long while since she had enjoyed even the smallest gallantry. She refrained, however, from returning the gesture with a curtsey, although the instinct to do so felt altogether natural, here on this greening hillside. Instead, she hastily pulled the coronet from her hair, and merely nodded at the gentleman.

"Forgive me," he laughed. "I hope I have not dismayed you into silence with my ill-chosen whimsy! Whenever I come into the circle, though, the fairy folk seem to take hold of my good sense. For the most part, it is only Caliban here who must usually endure my ravings."

"Do you suppose yourself to be Ariel, then?" she asked with mock incredulity.

"Alas, no," he returned, "a mere creature of flesh and bone. A very Ferdinand, I am afraid— which must, perforce, make you Miranda!"

"Perhaps," she replied, at last allowing a smile to form, "but I am very much afraid it is Miranda in later years."

"Ah, yes," he said speculatively. "I can see you are a veritable crone."

"I should have thought the realms of faerie would have taught you to distrust appearances," she replied. "For aught you know, I am a cruel hag, who will by my enchantment bind you to the circle."

He laughed at this, his eyes crinkling as he did so. "I do not fear unkind enchantments here— good Caliban would never let me fall prey to such."

At the mention of his name, the dog panted up at his master and wagged his tail.

"Caliban— an unusual name for an unusual animal," Marianne remarked. "How came he to lose his limb?"

The gentleman's brow furrowed. "I confess, I do not know. I found him thus, cast aside in a ditch where he had crawled to die, I suppose."

"Poor Caliban," she murmured. "It was good in you to take him— and see him mended."

He shook his head. "I had no choice— do but look into his eyes. To resist his appeal was beyond my poor powers, I assure you! And it was as much my good fortune as his, for it is an unhappy circumstance to be without such a boon companion."

Marianne glanced down at the black folds of her garment, then back up at him.

"I beg your pardon, madam," the gentleman sputtered abashedly, his eyes seeming for the first time to take in the evidence of her mourning. "Your gown . . . I had not considered . . ."

"Do not worry yourself," she said softly. "You intended no offense."

He shook his head. "I find I must worry whenever I discover I have been a boor!"

"You have hardly been that!" she protested. "Merely a little . . . blind, shall we say?"

"You are too kind, madam."

Marianne realized with a sudden regret that all vestiges of whimsy and lightness of humor had deserted him, and the stiffness of formal manners cloaked him now. Such was the effect of widowhood, she realized. Such it should be, too, and she would have to live with it. Besides, the very notion of engaging in a flirtation, however fleeting or innocent, ought to have appalled rather than attracted her. Where was her good sense now? To cover her embarrassment, she knelt beside the dog and scratched him about the throat and behind the ears.

"Come, Caliban," the gentleman said stiffly, "before we disgrace ourselves further."

He bowed again and bid her good day, then left her to her solitude among the rocks and sky.

When Marianne returned home, she made her way at once to her chamber. She had become accustomed to resting in the afternoon, but today, though a weariness had settled over her, she felt too restless to lie down. Images of her encounter on the hillside circled about her head, and she knew sleep would not come to her. She was annoyed with herself for allowing fancy to take possession of her. Was it not just such romantic notions which had once before led her to destruction? She could have no time, no thought for such things, she told herself sternly. The sooner she forgot the episode, the better.

She turned her mind with an effort toward other things. There were still one or two trunks she had not unpacked, which she might attend to. She had avoided the task really, for they contained the only mementos of her former life she had brought with her. It had been her intention to store the trunks away in the attic until some later, indeterminate time, but she had delayed consigning them there and told the maid she would eventually deal with them herself. The smaller of these drew her eye, and she knew she must look into it, if only to rejoice that its contents no longer bound her to the past. Perhaps, now she had made her escape, the spectre of yesterday would have lost its power.

She took a small key from a box on her dressing table, turned it in the trunk's lock, then paused. It was, she knew, the sound of her past on a stranger's lips which had prompted her in this endeavor. How strange to think she had come all this distance and still met with an experience which acted as a mirror to all she had abandoned, to all which had abandoned her.

Though she had not disturbed the contents since she had packed them away those many years ago, the clasp sprang to easily, and the perfume of lavender filled the air. What an odd sort of girl she must have been, she sighed, to trouble with sweet scents as she packed away her painful little tokens.

Several objects wrapped in tissue lay on the top layer, and she unwrapped them one by one. The first proved to be a little silk fan. The ivory sticks had yellowed somewhat, but when she opened it up, the painted scene was still clear: Daphne pursued by Apollo. She had forgot that image, but how ironic it had proved to be. If only, when she had found herself importuned and without power, some kindly god had troubled to change her into a laurel tree, when she cried out for aid.

If only.

Sometimes she felt her whole life were made up of regrets beginning with that phrase, and any wisdom she had gained, purchased with it.

She set the fan aside and unwrapped another piece. It was her tuzzy-muzzy, a small mother-of-pearl cone which still bore the dry remnants of a floral tribute. She had worn it pinned at her shoulder that last ball of her only season, her heart a-flutter at having received such a lovely nosegay from a gentleman well beyond her reach.

She had met the Marquis de la Roche the pre-

vious evening at a musicale, and flattered herself that she had charmed him a little. She knew,
however, that she was but a green girl, and he
a bored French aristocrat— or so she had
thought— one of the lucky ones whose family
had fled the Continent with fortune intact. It
was enough that he had danced with her, requested another, and retreated with an ironic
half-smile when her mother had denied him
that honor. The next morning brought the little
bouquet, tied up with pale pink ribbons: lady's
slipper, jonquil, a few buds of China rose.

What, she had fretted, was she to make of
such choices? She had knit her brow as she
pored over a small tract entailing the language
of flowers, as she and her schoolmates had
termed it. When she looked into it that morning, the little book offered several intriguing in-
terpretations of such a floral message. The
China rose was clear enough: beauty always new.
The jonquil, however, implied that the sender
begged a return of his affections, even his passion. The lady's slipper meant fickleness. Surely
he did not think of her thus. It was her mother,
not she, who had denied him further dances
that evening.

What a silly little innocent she had been!

Marianne set the tuzzy-muzzy aside and unwrapped a dance card. The names were still
clear, too clear. She tossed the card aside and
pressed her hands to her eyes. The scene appeared before her as bright, as sharply defined
as a waking dream. White-gowned maidens

stepped their way through the intricate figures of the Boulanger like snowflakes fluttering among rows of stiff dark trees. Her own gown was white as well, overlain with a demi-skirt of silver tissue, embroidered with dragonflies. The flowers she had received did not really suit the ensemble— the white roses and lily of the valley sent by another admirer would have done much better— but she would wear them anyway. She remembered looking down at her little silver slippers peeping from beneath her skirts, feeling her toes curl with anticipation.

When the first set was done, a collage of faces had greeted her as a host of young men approached to seek introductions. Before any could be accepted, however, she had heard a voice behind her:

"Good evening, my dear Miss Gardiner."

Marianne felt a rush of emotions as she recognized the lilting accent of the Marquis de la Roche. Her mother stiffened and briefly nodded her head at the gentleman. Marianne bit her lower lip with vexation. Mama's rudeness was not to be borne— even if she did not view the marquis as an eligible parti, there were other ways she might discourage his attentions.

"I have come to claim your daughter, Mrs. Gardiner," he continued, bowing over the older lady's hand. Marianne fought back the smile that twitched at the corners of her lips, as she watched a flush of annoyance flood her mother's countenance at the marquis's double-edged statement.

"*She was kind enough to promise she would stand up with me for this dance.*"

Marianne knew she had done no such thing, but before her mother could form a protest, she took the marquis's arm and followed him onto the dance floor, feeling somehow triumphant, even though she knew a whispered scolding would greet her when she was done. For the moment, it was enough that a handsome older man had claimed her hand, and that her mother could do nothing about it without causing a to-do.

The marquis led her out to the center of the room, and she felt the eyes of other women turn to her. He was tall and slim and elegant, his dark eyes lazy. Though her hands were, of course, gloved, his own curled around hers in a way that seemed intimate and proprietary. As her heart began to pace faster than the music, she charged herself sternly to be calm. Her finishing school manners were no match for his worldliness, she knew, but what harm could possibly come of a dance?

Before long they were weaving their way through the complicated figures of the set, meeting from time to time in promenade, then parting again as the lines divided. It was a good thing, she reflected, there was so little occasion for conversation, for she needed to concentrate on the steps of the dance. There was a great deal of difference between dancing with a master under the eye of her governess and elder sister, and performing for the starchy crowd that surrounded her now.

When next the line brought her to the marquis, he whispered, "Hold a moment."

Just then, an enormous crash came from across the ballroom. "Come with me, quickly."

The dance had brought them close to the French doors which led out to the garden and, as the rest of the assembly turned to see what had caused the disturbance, Marianne felt the marquis take her arm and twirl her out into the night. Above, a few clouds floated past the full moon, and the sky was spangled with stars. Beyond those luminaries, however, there was no light.

"I must return at once," she whispered hesitantly. "My mother will miss me directly."

"Let me look at you a moment in the moonlight, ma petite. You are so lovely in your silver gown— like some pretty trinket dropped from the moon's watch fob."

He took her face between his long elegant fingers and held it up. "So very beautiful."

"Please, my lord." She shrugged away from him, her heart beating wildly.

"Your mama has taken me in dislike, it seems, so I must steal my moments where I may. Be still a moment— I shall take you back. But I must watch for an opportunity so we shall not be remarked upon. Our escape I could arrange easily enough by bribing a footman to be clumsy— "

"You arranged . . . ?"

He laughed softly in the darkness. "You have caught my eye, chérie, and made me mad for

*you. There are other arrangements I have made
as well."*

"What do you mean?"

"Meet me tomorrow, and you will see."

*She did not immediately answer— such a re-
quest, of course, flew in the face of all she knew
was proper. Still, she could just catch the glint
of his eyes in the moonlight. Never before had
she felt such excitement. Through the window she
could see that the sedate groups of dancers had
reformed themselves and continued. She and the
marquis would soon be missed.*

*"Tomorrow, at four o'clock. The rose garden
at St. James Park," he said urgently, then swept
her back among the crowd.*

Marianne flung shut the lid of the trunk and
turned to the window to watch the sun sink
lower in the sky. She might flee to the ends of
the earth, but there were some things she would
never escape. Memory had not lost its razor's
edge, nor had her heart learned not to bleed.

Four

Though the next days continued blue and warm, Marianne did not again seek the stone circle. It was unlikely that another such encounter would take place, for surely the mysterious gentleman had found the meeting as uncomfortable as she. Despite her efforts to guard against thinking on it, she could not help but wonder who he was, and what had brought him to this remote district. There were neither estates nor lodges nearby which might attract parties for the hunting season, and certainly the district boasted no other diversions. Perhaps, she mused, the fairies had conjured him up out of memories they had read on her countenance. In any case, she was determined not to allow another such encounter, and stayed close to her house and garden.

Her mind, however, continued to wander, to find its way back to the magic of the stone circle. The thought of the gentleman's chivalry, however mistaken, often brought a small smile to her lips, as she sewed little gowns for her baby, or gathered the last of the roses. It could not hurt to dream a little, she told herself, as long as she reminded herself that was all it was. She had changed since she was a romantic girl, and knew the difference.

In her meandering dreams, she had no past, and she drew on childhood tales which sprang to mind these days as they had not done in many years. She was a part of the earth and air, got with child by some mysterious deity of the circle, and held there by a spell. Her enchantment might be broken only when some honest gentleman carried her beyond its domain. At night, before she fell to sleep, she turned to a worn volume of Shakespeare, and reread the magical words of *The Tempest*. When she shut her eyes to sleep, the image of the smiling gentleman in the circle arose before her, and the words of Miranda echoed, *How beauteous mankind is! O brave new world, that has such creatures in't!*

Still, dreams were dreams. By day she was Marianne and not Miranda. It was Marianne who pricked her finger as she pruned the roses, whose back ached, who wore drab colors and called herself a widow.

She was engaged one afternoon in the task of dividing some lily bulbs, when along the gravel path she heard the uneven approach of one of her servants.

"Beg pardon, ma'am," a soft voice came. "There's callers. Reverend and Mrs. Waller be asking if you're at leisure to receive."

Marianne looked up at the shy housemaid who stood at her side, and forced back a frown. She was indeed at her leisure, but receiving would definitely break up her peace. Nonetheless, the country was not the city, where the thinly veiled lie of "not at home" might keep visitors at bay. She would not turn them away.

"Oh, dear, Annie," she sighed, running a hand through the tresses which had escaped their pins. "I must be looking quite wild."

Annie shook her head diffidently, shifting from one foot to another. "Wild as a rose, and just as pretty, ma'am," she said with a blush.

Marianne arose slowly and brushed the dirt and grass from where it clung to her black skirts. "I declare, you will make me quite vain!" Glancing up, she smiled at the girl of whom she had already grown quite fond. Annie was herself a pretty little thing, but it was a great pity about her twisted leg. Thus encumbered, odds were she would never find a husband. No, she would spend her days in service in such houses as would overlook her infirmity. Perhaps, if all her plans continued to go well, Marianne could offer her a permanent position.

"Just give me a moment to steal up the back stairs," Marianne sighed, "then show them to the garden off the drawing room. Order tea, and I shall be down as quickly as I may."

Entertaining callers had not been part of Marianne's design when she first envisioned her country retreat, nor was it a common occurrence. Reverend Enos Waller and his wife, however, had taken it upon themselves to call almost every afternoon to see how she fared. When winter came, she knew she would be glad enough of their company, but for now she longed to savor her home and solitude— and the sense of privacy so indispensable to her as she embarked on this new life. Still, it was altogether possible they might let drop some hint as to who the gentleman of the circle was, and the truth— which experience had taught her was bound to be mundane— might help her tame her thoughts.

In her chamber, she untied the strings of her broad garden hat and flung it on the bed, then scrubbed the soil from her hands and bathed her face. It was still strange for her to see the plain furnishings reflected behind her in the mirror. Her simple bed was covered with a white counterpane. A bunch of daisies sat on the nightstand. Unlike the more ornate chamber she had used in London, the room looked modest and clean, almost like a nun's cell, she imagined.

She brushed her hair and pinned it up in a simple knot, then went to the wardrobe. Choosing another gown was not difficult, for they were all of them a sober black or gray and restrained in style— as befit a recent widow. Before too long, her toilette was complete, and a quick glance in the glass confirmed that she looked presentable.

When she joined her guests, she found Annie pouring out tea for them. As she nodded her dismissal to the servant, the reverend stood and bowed; meanwhile, his wife, far less constrained than he, took Marianne's hands in hers and pressed them. She was a pleasant woman of middle years, rather tall like her husband, with a long homely face and a quick smile.

"How very lovely you are today, Mrs. Glencoe. Quite blooming, do you not think, Enos?"

The reverend silently smiled his agreement.

"You must not mind my husband, Mrs. Glencoe," Mrs. Waller said with a laugh. "He has been busy thinking up tomorrow's sermon, and it must always put him in a pucker to try to discover words of four syllables with which to obscure quite simple thoughts. Trust me, Enos, the folk hereabouts would like you the better for speaking to them plainly."

"You make me sound an altogether priggish sort, Suzannah," he returned mildly, smiling a little at her teasing. "Mrs. Glencoe will not know what to think of me."

"Then best she judge for herself, I suppose," his helpmeet laughed. "Do you think you will feel well enough to attend services this week, Mrs. Glencoe?"

Marianne looked down for a moment. She had stayed away from church since her arrival, unsure whether she was equal to carrying her role so far. In many ways her new life seemed more true than the old; however, she did not wish to put herself to that particular test just yet. Would she enter the church doors only to discover guilt and a sense of hypocrisy flooding her heart? She had merely opened a trunk earlier in the week, and it had become a Pandora's box of emotions. Her life and happiness were so precious now, she could not bear to see them sullied again.

"It is difficult to say," she demurred at last. "You see, I am so often unwell in the morning.

One does not always know in advance, you see . . ."

"Oh, to be sure," Mrs. Waller interrupted, her tone immediately contrite. "How thoughtless of me to ask such a thing. But you are feeling more the thing, are you not? I must say, your color is much improved since first you arrived here."

At this remark, Marianne felt a rush of embarrassment flood to her cheeks. She did not in the least like discussing her delicate condition— certainly not considering its circumstances— in the presence of a clergyman, however ignorant he was of her true identity and history. She responded with a noncommittal nod, therefore, as she took a seat at Mrs. Waller's side.

"I must tell you, Mrs. Glencoe," Mrs. Waller went on hurriedly, handing her a cup of tea, "that our old friend Dr. Venables is returned to the village from Edinburgh. He has been away from the countryside this last month at least, has he not, Enos?"

"All of that, I imagine. We have missed him greatly, but I am sure it is to his credit that he travels to learn of new treatments and discoveries firsthand. Not only has he dedicated his talents to our poor parish, but he is one of the few physicians who does not deem it beneath him to perform surgery as well as diagnose. I only hope the villagers recognize how very fortunate we are to count such an excellent gentleman a part of our community."

"I am certain they must be," Marianne said, lowering her cup and stifling a sigh of disap-

pointment. Surely the doctor of whom they
spoke was a venerable old saint, not a golden-
haired apparition with mischievous eyes. Annie
had mentioned the doctor from time to time, as
well, in terms of such awe as must confirm his
identity as a graybeard.

The reverend and his wife exchanged a glance.
"There are those few who will always complain, however. Some who . . ." Mrs. Waller
searched for a word, "some who are determined
to be unhappy. And distrustful of strangers."

"Is he so newly come to Waite then?" Marianne asked.

"No, no," the reverend told her with an in-
dulgent smile. "Dr. Venables has been here
these ten years, quite as long as we."

Marianne raised her brows. Did the village, for
all its outward congeniality, consider her in the
same suspicious light? Clearly, they must. "As
long as that," she murmured, "and still dis-
trusted?"

"By a few," Mrs. Waller admitted. "But you
must know, that is not our case. Even though
Enos and I are late arrivals, the family is known
in these parts. The living here was held by an
uncle for some twenty-five years. When he
passed away, Enos was invited to take his place."

The reverend leaned forward and brushed a
stray lock of graying hair off his broad forehead,
in a gesture that reminded Marianne of an earnest schoolboy.

"Let me tell you a story our uncle once told
me, Mrs. Glencoe," he said kindly. "Uncle Eras-

mus once officiated at the funeral of a man who died here at the ripe age of eighty-four. But for the first month of his life, the deceased had lived in this village his entire span of years. However, when a neighbor stepped forward to speak the eulogy, he opened it thus, 'Gracious Lord, we pray you will embrace this stranger to our soil . . .' "

He broke off with a laugh, "An extreme case, perhaps, and it did take place some years ago, but you take my meaning. There are some, most, who will embrace the stranger to their hearts, and others who will always consider strangers . . . well, strangers."

Marianne looked from the husband to the wife. She certainly did not crave society for herself, nor even necessarily the goodwill of her neighbors. But a slight frisson of discomfort traced her spine. Not quite fear, yet akin to it. Distrust could lead to curiosity, and she did not, for her child's sake, wish her facade of respectability to be subjected to scrutiny.

"In whom, then," she asked after a long moment, "do they place their trust in matters of health, if not the doctor?"

Reverend Waller shook his head. "It depends on the ailment, of course. Most seek out the doctor, and he is quite willing to accept whatever they have to offer from their gardens or stock in payment. There are many who still call on Old Maggie, a so-called wise woman of these parts. I'm afraid some view the doctor in light of an upstart rival to her practice, one who ignores old wisdom. The two of them seem to rub along well enough, though, and even consult one another from time to time, or so I am told. You will see the old girl about, I am sure.

"But, pray, do not fret yourself with such fears," he went on. "You are not breaking into the order of the community, usurping power as it were, as poor Dr. Venables does. No one will think you an intruder."

"Merely an outsider," she said evenly. "And my child?"

Mrs. Waller touched her arm, and said softly, "A child born in Waite belongs to everyone— even the hardest of skeptics."

Marianne looked down, following her guest's gaze, and realized her hands were clasped protectively around the slight swell beneath her breasts. She released her breath, allowing her hands to unclench, and folded them demurely on her lap.

Giving her husband a significant look, Mrs. Waller said, "Pray, Mrs. Glencoe, let us, you and I, take a turn in your lovely garden. All too soon it will have faded, and I should like to store up pictures of it to take me through the winter. I think perhaps Enos would like to sit quietly for a while, and contemplate his words of wisdom for this Sunday."

"You must forgive me, Mrs. Glencoe," Mrs. Waller began as soon as they had left her husband behind. "How unthinking I was just now. I know you will come to services as soon as you are able. It is merely that I am anxious to see more of you. There are so few here with whom I can chat so comfortably as I can with you. It is good to at last have a friend.''

Marianne took her hand and squeezed it. She had not thought what a lonely life Mrs. Waller must live with her quiet husband. It would be such a blessing to share a friendship, but Marianne feared an intimacy might arise— and that intimacy might prompt her to reveal more of herself than was wise.

From behind a trellised screen came the rasping sound of scissors, as one of the servants snipped away at herbs in the kitchen garden. The scent of freshly cut mint and marjoram wafted toward her on the breeze.

"It smells heavenly," Mrs. Waller sighed, breaking the awkward silence. "I have had little luck with herbs in my own garden."

"These were cultivated by some earlier tenant," Marianne told her, "so I can take no credit. They have proved a godsend, however— these last weeks, I find myself craving more seasoning in my food. Mrs. Bridges thinks me quite heathen, I am afraid, when I season her good plain food with pinches of this and that."

"I am sure she cannot," Mrs. Waller assured her. "She must know the fancies of women in your condition are to be humored."

"Perhaps, but I am afraid I shall soon test her patience. Some years ago, I tasted an Indian dish called curry. I did not care for it at the time, for it is quite fiery you know, but I find myself unaccountably longing for it now."

"Another reason to celebrate Dr. Venables's return, Mrs. Glencoe. I seem to recall he has traveled in the East—perhaps he will have an idea of how it is made."

"Ah! But is the gentleman to be trusted?" Marianne asked with mock incredulity. "We must not forget poor Rapunzel's mother."

Mrs. Waller looked at her blankly.

"Surely you remember the old tale," Marianne said, a little chagrined at having spoken her odd thought aloud. "The queen, who was with child, found herself suffering a formidable hunger for rampion— which, as luck would have it, grew only in the garden of a neighboring witch. The bargain they struck is not one I would care for."

"Of course, the rash promise! I had forgot all about that story," her new friend laughed. "But I hardly think the doctor will demand your firstborn child in exchange for a dish of curry. I cannot guarantee, however, he will not seek to enlist your help in one of his many charitable projects."

"What do you mean?"

In the distance just then, the unhurried *clop* and *whir* of a horse and curricle could be heard drawing near.

"I believe that may be the doctor now," Mrs. Waller announced. "I shall call to him—then you may see for yourself."

Five

Mrs. Waller approached the fence and, leaning over it, waved a hand. "Dr. Venables!" she cried. "Do stop a moment with us."

As the curricle slowed to a halt, Marianne stepped back, feeling suddenly and unreasonably shy. It was foolish, she knew, but the notion of slipping silently and quickly away appealed to her enormously. She had not felt thus when she first met the Reverend Waller and his wife, but the nature of that acquaintance could remain as distant as she liked. With a doctor it would necessarily be different. Regardless of the man himself, the inevitable relationship between patient and doctor was sure to encompass an uncomfortable combination of emotional distance and invasive physicality— very like those connections which had ruled her life these last years. Taking a deep breath, she made a deliberate effort to fold her hands calmly in front of her, and assume at least the appearance of composure.

"Good morning, my dear Mrs. Waller!" the doctor's voice came through the shrubbery. Marianne felt her pulse race as she recognized the voice. Her gentleman of the stone circle and the doctor were indeed one and the same. But how could that be? Vanished were the visions of the venerable, gray-bearded physician, but how might the gentleman who had flirted and spoken of fairies step into that rigid role? It did not seem possible.

"You look very like a blossom, Mrs. Waller, peeking from among those blooms," the doctor went on. "Be careful of those who would gather you up!"

"And a very odd sort of blossom that must be," Mrs. Waller replied with tart good humor. It seemed she was accustomed to his flirtatious manner. "Perhaps you ought take to spectacles before long. But come, you must make the acquaintance of our new neighbor, Mrs. Glencoe."

Mrs. Waller turned and took Marianne by the hand, leading her to the gate, just as the doctor came through it. He surveyed her with sparkling eyes, and a smile flooded his face, hiding his scar in its creases.

"My pleasure, Mrs. Glencoe."

Marianne nodded mutely as he took her hand in his and pressed it warmly. For a fleeting moment, she had expected him to bow over it, but the gallant gentleman of yesterday had, it seemed, assumed country manners.

Though the doctor released her hand almost at once, his eyes caught hers in a clear, direct way and held them. Immediately, she felt as if she were being studied in these new surroundings, assessed, though she knew not quite how.

Perhaps he was casting her in another light, as she was him, in the face of reality.

"I had already planned to call here today or tomorrow," he said with a smile, "for I must look in on your Annie, but I am glad to be made known to you."

She noticed he avoided saying he was glad to "make her acquaintance," for that would have denied their former meeting. Mrs. Waller would never know that they had previously encountered one another, and for some reason Marianne was glad of it.

"So, you have been returned but a day and already the local gossips have been hard at work, doctor," Mrs. Waller laughed. "London will not have prepared you for these parts, Mrs. Glencoe. I would not be surprised to learn Doctor Venables not only knew which of his patients is employed in your household, but has also heard a variety of appraisals of your own situation."

Marianne looked at the doctor curiously.

"I am afraid Mrs. Waller has the right of it, Mrs. Glencoe," he said, shaking his head ruefully. "Indeed, I had not been one half hour in my own parlor before three worthy ladies had called to advise me that I must look in on you before long. I hope you are not offended by their forwardness?"

"Not at all," Marianne was able to reply after a moment. "It is true, I am used to living a quiet sort of life, quite unremarked on by my neighbors— but I am sure it was very kind in them to show interest in a solitary widow."

Something in the doctor's gaze forced Marianne to avert her eyes at the untruth of her statement. No one else had questioned her veracity— why should he? Oh, how she would like to remain unremarked upon the rest of her days! How odd if anyone should discern that these last weeks had been the happiest, most serene she had experienced in many years. However, the less said, she decided, the fewer suspicions raised.

"And have you been well?" he asked, still studying her face.

Indeed she had been for the most part, but now that Marianne had used the excuse of ill health to avoid Mrs. Waller's invitations to attend services, she hardly felt she could say as much in the lady's presence. Still, it would never do to tell such an untruth to the doctor, for who knew what odd remedies he would insist she imbibe?

"Well enough," she replied in tones she hoped, rather wryly, Mrs. Waller would interpret as long-suffering. "It is good of you to concern yourself with Annie, when you are so recently returned, doctor. Perhaps you will call again when you are more at your leisure?"

The doctor glanced quickly in the direction of Mrs. Waller, then smiled again at Marianne. "I must own my schedule is quite full today, and it will grow dark sooner than I would like."

So, the gentleman's intuition was not to be faulted. How singular! "Thank you," she murmured.

"Tomorrow afternoon will do very well, however," he continued, "if it will not interrupt your household schedule. Annie is a particular favorite of mine, and I have found something I think will alleviate some of the distress of her infirmity."

It seemed odd that one of his class should interest himself in a servant. She hoped indeed it was no more than professional concern, but her past had made her distrustful of the motives of all men. Bereft of a likely excuse, however, she could not but agree to his proposal, and breathed a sigh of relief as the conversation returned to other subjects. For the next several minutes, the doctor and Mrs. Waller engaged in a conversation of inconsequentials, for little of note appeared to have taken place since last these two met, and it was not long before Marianne was left once again with her friend.

"It seems I have escaped my first encounter unscathed," Marianne commented as they returned their steps toward the house. Mrs. Waller looked at her narrowly. "From your earlier warning, I had thought to be embroiled in a dozen worthy projects by now."

"Perhaps I exaggerated a little," Mrs. Waller replied with a smile, "but did you not note the appraising eye with which he observed you? To be sure, he is already formulating questions to ask when he calls tomorrow, which will ascertain the best use of you in his charitable undertakings."

Marianne raised her eyebrows. "Are not such

things more rightly your husband's concern?" she asked.

Mrs. Waller sighed. "Enos is a good man," she said quietly, "but his interests are . . . intellectual. I am sorry he did not find a living which placed him close to a university. His mental powers, I am afraid, are frustrated here. There are few to appreciate his fine sermons; poor Enos had far rather delineate fine points about the nature of God than puzzle long over the nature of man in this world God made."

From where they stood in the garden, they could see Reverend Waller bent over the book he had brought with him, oblivious to his surroundings.

"Do not mistake me," Mrs. Waller continued hastily. "I do not mean to criticize my husband. He is who he is, and I make amends where I can for his lack of interest in the village. I merely feel sorry his life fell thus. And for his people, too. They are not . . ." She paused a moment. "They are not well suited, he and they."

The nature of God and man. The duties of each person toward his fellows. These were questions Marianne had pondered very little during her youth, and assiduously avoided in her adulthood. The one thing her darker musings had led her to believe, however, was that if there were in fact a God, he had no love for women, and little for any other creature. She sighed. Another thought she must keep to herself.

* * *

Although weariness settled over her like a heavy cloak, Marianne found that when the night came, it brought her little sleep; when she did from time to time drift off, the events of the previous days wound themselves into a tangled skein of odd annoying dreams. She found herself entering a ballroom, dressed in her widow's weeds; Reverend Waller sat at the pianoforte where he played a rambling tune with one hand, and held a dusty philosophical work in the other. Her parents were there, too, somehow, sitting at the edge of the room in high-backed chairs; when their eyes met hers, they smiled at her and nodded impassively, as if she were merely another stranger. Perhaps, as such, they would accept her. She approached and dipped in a low curtsey, bowing her head before them.

"Come, girl," she heard her father say gruffly. "There is no call for this sort of formality from one who was never born!"

Turning slowly away, she perused the dance floor. There she spotted her sister Olivia, twirled through the crowd by a masterful hand, her white gown swirling and fluttering like a blossom on the breeze. Marianne's heart froze. Olivia was dancing with the Marquis de la Roche. She must stop them, save her sister. She pushed forward, and those gathered about began to laugh and whisper to one another. A woman's voice drifted to her, "What a singular *creature!*"

From the edges of the dream, Mrs. Waller

hurried to her side, whispering, "Really, Mrs. Glencoe, what on earth can you be thinking of? How can you go about wearing such a thing?"

But why ever not? she wondered. Did no one remember she was in mourning? Then she looked down, only to discover she was wearing, not the black in which she had entered, but her maiden gown, white and silver, hanging in shreds over a thin chemise.

Marianne sat up in bed and pressed her hands to her cheeks. Her old nurse had always held that in dreams lay hidden messages and portents. Did this dream prefigure the exposure she feared? Or did it merely reflect her uncertainties? Probably the latter, she felt sure, for she had taken great care to achieve and protect her facade.

She shook her head in the darkness. Her sister would not give her away, she knew, and only the oddest twist of fate could bring about disclosure now. But what if she had overlooked some small thing, any clue which might betray her? No, she told herself sternly. She had been over every detail, time and time again.

She turned about restlessly in the tangled sheets. It was no good. Though sleep might come in fragments, it would not bring repose. Pulling back her bed curtains, she spied the first gray light of dawn outlining the windows. Arise, she thought, and greet the day betimes. Lying abed fretting would achieve nothing.

It was the doctor, her stranger in the circle, she decided, who had so unsettled her. The echo of the *ton* in Venables's voice, his manner, both yesterday and in their previous meeting, must have unnerved her more than she imagined. In a single moment, the world she had tried to escape walked calmly into her little haven and fixed her with a speculative gaze.

It was not merely the doctor, however. She knew it had been a bad idea to open that trunk, that Pandora's box. A swarm of stinging memories were unleashed and still buzzed about her head. A foolish, foolish notion to think she could bear the past. She would have the trunk stored away in the attic after all.

Sighing heavily, she swung to an upright position, but was forced to sit still a moment, clutching the edge of the bed, as the room spun about and her stomach lurched. It would pass in a moment, she knew, but muttered an oath nonetheless that she should once again have forgot to arise slowly. She sat quietly, counting to ten, waiting for the floor to solidify beneath her feet, for the rising ache of sickness to dissipate. Gone were her idle dreams of the previous week.

Thank God she was alone, she thought, that at least there was no man snoring beside her, oblivious to her discomfort. Eve's curse, indeed! How married women must despise their husbands throughout pregnancies!

Still, she reflected, Olivia did not seem to do so. She had borne William two children, carried now a third, and knew far better than Marianne what trials were yet to come. But her sister's face still lit up at the mention of her husband's name. Bearing children truly seemed a blessing to her— not an Old Testament curse. Marianne shook her head. Olivia's life, her way of viewing the world, could never be hers. She was grateful enough for the happiness she had thus far gleaned.

After a moment or two, Marianne once again felt equal to facing the day and, pulling a shawl over her nightrail, descended the staircase and ventured out into the garden. To the east, the sunlight had barely begun to creep above the horizon, while the western sky was still illuminated by the setting of a full moon. The air was full of the scent of daybreak: wet grass and fertile earth. Herbs from the kitchen garden, just beyond the hedge, perfumed the air as if they had been newly cut. Marianne breathed deeply, relishing the tonic effect of the morning.

The birds, too, had come to life, singing, squabbling among themselves; she was acquainted with their voices now, although she could not have put a name to many. There was this morning, though, an unfamiliar rasp which, for a moment blended with the birds' songs. Almost immediately, however, she realized that the sound was mechanical, man-made. The rasp of scissors. Was the kitchen girl about already, gathering herbs? She must be, for now Marianne realized that the scent of mint and lemon grass on the breeze was far more pungent than it ought to have been in the stillness of morning.

Mystified, she stepped carefully along the dimly lit path, around the hedge and into the kitchen garden. There, a bent figure snipped away at a bunch of rosemary, filling a basket as she went. It was a woman, elderly by the rigidity of her movements, but not one of her household staff. Marianne stood watching curiously as daybreak continued to illuminate the scene.

Six

"Good morrow to you, mistress." The woman broke the silence without looking up. She cut a few more sprigs and placed them in her basket as Marianne looked on. "I see you've come to heal yourself on the dawn's good air. Naught better for what ails a body, even if 'tis nothing more than a child coming on."

Marianne still said nothing, but watched as the intruder, for such she was, straightened herself and set her basket on the flagstones. "Come then, mistress. Let an old woman see your young face."

She should have been affronted at such forwardness, but, without knowing why she did so, Marianne stepped further into the garden. The woman came to her, took Marianne's chin between her long fingers, and turned her face to the rising sun.

"Pretty thing," she whispered. "Sadness and happiness both in your eyes. Secrets— do not worry, I'll not pry—and dreams. Wiser than I thought at first." She dropped her hand and cocked her head a moment. "You'll do. But 'twas more than the morning ills sent you early from your bed, aye?"

Marianne felt a sudden stab of fear at these words. Who was this singular person? How could she see into Marianne's heart, and what did she know of secrets? The woman stood observing her closely, like a sharp-eyed wren. Then yesterday's conversation with the Wallers came back to her. "You are called Maggie, are you not?"

"Aye. Old Maggie. And you wonder— isn't it true?— what she does trespassing here?" The old woman chuckled softly. "The earth knows nothing of boundaries, mistress, and neither does Maggie. The herbs and flowers call out to be gathered, so I oblige them."

Although the old woman's presence in her garden had for a moment disturbed Marianne, she discovered, to her surprise, a sense of calm descending over her as she listened. Maggie, whatever her odd ways, had a kind voice and gentle manner. "Come, sit with me a moment," she heard herself say.

"A moment, as you say," Maggie returned. "We shall bid the old moon a good night, and watch the sun take its place in the sky."

They found a bench and sat together, watching the sky grow golden. As the day brightened, Marianne studied her companion. Though her hair was silver, the face it framed was virtually unlined. Though her hands showed evidence of hard work, the fingers were long and elegant.

Though her speech was countrified, she expressed herself well. A puzzle.

It was a puzzle, too, Marianne reflected, that she should choose to indulge this company, to occupy herself thus. None of her previous acquaintances would understand it. Perhaps it was that, in her new anonymity, she could allow some measure of freedom to the woman, to the self, who had lived submerged beneath the various facades the years had dictated for her. The virginal girl, the fallen woman, had merely been pretenses, invented and donned at the charge of others. Now, she might at last do as she pleased, even to the point of eccentricity, and it pleased her to greet the gentle morning with this odd woman beside her.

"Tell me something of the herbs," she said finally. "What are their properties and virtues?"

Maggie plucked a stem of rosemary and bruised the leaves between her fingers. A spicy fragrance filled the air.

"You ask far more than I can give this morning, mistress. Herb lore is a life's work, not a moment's fancy. This little sprig alone," Maggie said, holding it up, "can be treated in diverse ways— dried, made into tinctures, decoctations for diverse complaints. Tell me— do you wish to learn, or are you merely talking?"

Marianne considered for a time. In truth, she did not know. Was it the herbs, or the woman herself which interested her more? Or perhaps it was merely this moment in time, this respite between fevered dreams and the start of another day, that conferred a fascination to the woman beside her.

Marianne looked up to see Maggie studying her. The old woman nodded her head sagely. "You are wise to ponder this well. Herb lore becomes a life all in itself, and there's not often room for others. Still, I may tell you a thing or two, from time to time, as our paths cross."

Marianne smiled. "In exchange for my herbs?"

"You may think of it that way, if you choose," the older woman said. Turning, she placed a hand on Marianne's stomach and held it there a moment. "She will be here well in time for Yule, God willing."

Marianne felt a glimmer of relief. A tension of which she had only dimly been aware disappeared. "She?"

Maggie nodded. "And a daughter is always a gift. Take a draft of valerian tea before bed each night," she said, as she stood and lifted her basket, "and dream of new love and your sweet baby, not silliness."

A daughter. A gift. If only she might rely on Old Maggie's prediction, Marianne thought. She had envisioned her babe as a girl child. A smiling daughter whom she might raise and watch grow into the woman she might have been. She had even imagined gowns and hair ribbons. Naturally, she had known she was just as likely to bear a son, but she had turned her mind from such an eventuality without examining why she did so.

Should Cheswick somehow discover her condition, she knew that, despite the child's illegitimacy, the notion of his fathering a son would be of more consequence than a daughter. But was it more than that? Was it, she wondered, because she feared herself? Could she, who had seen her life transformed at the whims of men, raise a son without polluting his small world with her prejudice? Could she raise a son according to her own ideals, who would then be able to negotiate the turbulent waters of a world created by and for men?

A daughter, she thought. Please, a daughter.

By afternoon, the tranquility of her morning encounter had passed to memory, and Marianne sat anxiously in the drawing room as she awaited Dr. Venables's arrival. The palms of her hands were cold and moist, despite the day's warmth. The pleasant room which had been a comfort to her these last weeks did not now seem a sanctuary.

She did not have a clear sense of what the doctor's visit might mean. Would he assume, because of her condition, that she wished an examination? Or would he pay a simple call, turn his attention to Annie, and wait for her to request his services? In one sense, she looked forward to the former, for she was impatient to ascertain whether the child she carried progressed as it should. The notion of such intimate scrutiny, however, distressed her inordinately. The thought of such self-revelation was misery.

She glanced about the room nervously and nodded to herself, satisfied. She had done her best to see that her furnishings revealed only her taste, no more. No clues to her history, she felt sure, could be discerned there.

But her body? Was it true, as some suggested, that one's past could be read there? Surely this must be an exaggeration, but she remembered, with a shudder, being told by one of her gentlemen that her body seemed "well suited to love." She had not quite known what he had meant, nor had she asked, but she worried now. Could clues to what she had been be visible to a trained, perceptive eye?

There must be another alternative. Surely Maggie was a midwife. Surely she would serve as well as the doctor, Marianne told herself. She would merely tell the doctor she had made arrangements with the old woman. The possibility of his taking offense at such a pronouncement was less daunting than the idea of his intruding on her privacy.

She heard the rise and fall of voices in the passage just then, and she steeled herself to the encounter, sought to convey a more composed demeanor than she truly felt. A tap came at the door and Annie entered, followed closely by the doctor who carried a basket over his arm.

"It's Dr. Venables come to call, ma'am, but only look at me!" The girl walked carefully across the room before her and turned, smiling broadly. "My limp— it is all but gone!"

"How wonderful!" Marianne exclaimed. Truly, the girl's infirmity seemed barely visible. She glanced at the doctor, but could not catch his eye. "But what— ?"

"He's worked a miracle, that's what," Annie declared, nodding at the doctor, "and I do not know how I will ever thank him."

At these words, Marianne saw Venables's face tighten, as an expression very like pain crossed over it. How odd! Most men would glow in the light of such praise. He seemed unwilling to even hear it.

The doctor shook his head. "You must not say such things, Annie." He glanced at Marianne, his face still drawn. "I have done very little besides bring her a new shoe, Mrs. Glencoe. Its sole is built up, you see, so that her limbs are made more equal."

Annie made tutting sounds, as if to admonish the man's modesty.

"However, you must be careful, Annie," he went on, as he seemingly recovered himself, "to accustom yourself to using this device gradually. Otherwise, I fear your back will begin to ache."

Annie frowned in apparent confusion. "What has my back to do with *this?*" she asked, lifting the edge of her skirt to reveal the toe of her new shoe.

"Many afflictions take their toll on the back, Annie— and even some conditions which are not quite afflictions." He turned to Marianne with a wry smile. "Is that not correct, Mrs. Glencoe?"

Marianne nodded tentatively. It was true, her back had never hurt before these last months. Now she sometimes felt as if she had spent her day carrying boulders about.

"Bring us tea, please, Annie," Marianne said.

"Oh, and a saucer of warm milk, if you please," the doctor added. He grinned sheepishly at Marianne as Annie left to perform her duties. "I've brought you something— I hope you will not take it amiss, Mrs. Glencoe, and that it will be a welcome gift."

He picked up the basket he had brought and carried it to Marianne. She took it in her hands, and glanced up at him. He wore the expression of a hopeful schoolboy. She turned once more to the basket before her and lifted the cover.

A huddle of kittens, black, orange, and gray-striped, stared back at her through wide unblinking eyes. She caught her breath. Mama and Papa had never allowed her or Olivia to keep pets when they were children, and she had forgot until now how she had once longed for a kitten or puppy.

"They are hardly bigger than my fist," she whispered. "How old are they?"

"About three weeks, as nearly as I can tell," he told her. "They have just lost their mama to a stoat, and I am afraid my Caliban will not countenance their being brought into my house. They must now be fed by hand, you see, if they are to survive. I have lost the runt already, poor little calico. It occurred to me that perhaps you would not mind . . ."

Marianne shook her head quickly. Of course, she did not mind. "Look! They have eyes like little pansies. Sweethearts! What are they called?"

He smiled back at her and knelt at her side. "That is for you to decide," he told her. "I generally opt for something lofty and Shakespearean— I believe a noble name is important for all creatures— but it must be entirely up to you."

"I see. Like Caliban. So it was you yourself who saw to the mending of his injury?"

The doctor frowned. "I do not believe in accidents, Mrs. Glencoe, so when I found him and saw he was still alive, I knew I could not leave him thus. I must do something for him. I applied what I knew of humans to the fellow. What remained of his leg had to be cut off, but I stitched the wound well, and he has thrived despite the infirmity."

She looked at him with new respect. There were few so kind of heart; fewer still who would thus burden themselves. Just then, Annie returned with the tea tray and a small dish of milk. How did the girl figure in all of this, she wondered? Another stray to be looked after?

The doctor took the milk from her, then sat beside Marianne. "You must dip the corner of a napkin into the milk, then let each one suck what it may. There," he said, as he brushed the mouth of a gray-striped fellow, "you see. This one has already learned what to expect."

She laughed as the kitten sucked hungrily and

kneaded the proffered napkin with its claws. "That one must surely be called Falstaff!"

"Capital— he is a fine fat fellow. And the little ginger-colored one?"

Marianne traced its back with a tentative finger. "It is so little and forlorn— Ophelia, do you think?"

He picked it up gently and, turning it over, made a cursory examination. "Yes, it is a little maid. Ophelia will serve very well."

"Poor little one," Marianne sighed as she gazed at the kitten. It was sniffing the air blindly, attempting to find the source of the scent of milk. "Will she survive, do you think?"

"If her brother can be persuaded to share, there is no reason why she should not."

She frowned a moment, then said, "Annie, fetch a pair of gloves for me— and be sure they are kid, not silk. I have an idea," she said, as the maid went off to do her mistress's bidding. "I do not know if it will serve, but I can at least try. They are so sweet and innocent, are they not?"

The doctor shook his head ruefully. "Wait until they are old enough to wreak havoc on your sewing basket. Then I shall ask you."

Marianne dipped a finger in the milk and brushed it across the newly christened Ophelia's mouth. A tiny pink tongue emerged, and the kitten licked eagerly.

"Yes," the doctor chuckled, "she will do quite well."

He put his own finger into the milk and began to feed the third kitten. Marianne looked up and caught him smiling at her, and felt the heat rise to her cheeks. Somehow, the kittens' nursing motions made the task of feeding seem an altogether more intimate endeavor. She looked down quickly and remained intent on her task, until Annie entered again with a pair of gloves.

"Thank you, Annie," she murmured. "Will you hand me my sewing basket now?"

Annie watched, horrified, as Marianne tied off two fingers and poked the end of each of the remaining three with a large darning needle. "Oh, madam!" she protested. "Have you gone and ruined your fine gloves for these little gluttons? Surely a pair of old Martin's work gloves would have done as well."

Abandoned for a moment while Marianne pursued her task, the kittens mewed reproachfully. "Tyrants! Hush now. They have delicate little mouths, you see, Annie," she said softly. "They will do far better if they do not have to fight to get a few drops of milk. They would wear themselves out trying to suck through canvas."

She picked up the saucer of milk and carefully poured it into the glove. Then she arranged it among the tyrants, so each had its own finger. At first, they did not seem to understand what they must do. "Oh, dear," she whispered. "Perhaps I was wrong. But I had thought— "

"Half a moment," Dr. Venables interrupted. He took one of the milk-filled fingers, placed it firmly against Falstaff's mouth, and pressed. A stream of milk splashed in its face. The kitten looked startled, but at once licked the milk off its face and began to search for more. Before long, it was sucking milk under its own power. The doctor repeated this operation with each of the others. Only Ophelia still had difficulty. "Well," he said after a moment, "some learn more slowly than others."

"I shall keep trying," she said. "How often ought they to be fed?"

"Oh, no more than six or seven times a day, I imagine."

"Six or seven— ?" she gasped.

"Indeed," he returned with a nod. "And very good practice you will find it for when you have a babe of your own demanding his dinner."

"Her dinner, if you please!" Marianne corrected with asperity.

"Ah! Are you convinced of such a thing then?" he asked, raising an eyebrow at her. "I hope you may not be disappointed."

As Marianne returned his gaze, she thought she detected some puzzlement therein, and perhaps even a hint of reproof. "I shall not be disappointed, I assure you, in any healthy child. It is just that I have longed so for a daughter, and Old Maggie has assured me— "

"Ah!" the doctor broke in. "Old Maggie, is it then? You may be assured indeed, for I have not heard that her predictions have ever gone amiss."

Marianne realized that now, when Maggie's

name had obtruded into the conversation, was the very time to inform him of her decision. She took a deep breath. "I hope you may be right. She told me so this very morning, when I discovered her in my garden snipping herbs as bold as you please."

"You must not mind Maggie's odd ways," Venables began.

"Indeed, I do not," Marianne said in a rush. "She is a redoubtable woman, and I have asked her to attend me when my time comes."

A mere pulse beat or two might have passed before the doctor replied, "You are fortunate in your choice, I am sure. I have heard naught but good of her skills as a healer and midwife." He smiled at her then. "Do not think I will be offended, Mrs. Gardiner. Most women, I am sure, are more comfortable with one of their own at hand, when their time comes."

Marianne felt a rush of relief at these words, for he did not appear to have taken her decision amiss. Though their acquaintance had been brief and, for the most part, unsettling, she would not like to offend this good man. She glanced down at the kittens. They were sleeping peacefully, nestled in their basket like a trio of variegated pussy willows. When she looked up again, the doctor was smiling at her still.

Seven

As he drove home that afternoon, Dr. Venables found his mind returning again and again to his call at Rosewood Cottage. That was not entirely unexpected, however. He had not stopped thinking of its mistress since he first encountered her in the stone circle. He had found his way to that enchanted place immediately on his return from Edinburgh. The legends of virgins turned to stone might terrify the villagers into forsaking its environs, but he found the circle peaceful, and always left it with a lighter heart and a renewed sense of hope. Now that sense of hope had become personified.

The image of Mrs. Glencoe, crowned with flowers, had possessed him ever since he first spied her. Most women would have looked foolish thus arrayed, but she did not. She looked utterly natural, as if she were one of the fairy folk believed to inhabit the region.

It was little wonder that he had not immediately noticed her widow's weeds. Her face invited the eye like a cameo framed in silk. Her movements were liquid, her form gently feminine. She was undeniably beautiful, achingly beautiful. But there was an intriguing mystery about her as well, which held his mind in thrall.

To begin with, he was almost certain he remembered something of her from his previous life in the *ton*. Her face and manner, at any rate. Her family name would doubtless come in time, whether he wished it or not. For all his efforts, he was still unable to purge the myriad memories of his former life in that glittering superficial circle.

Mrs. Glencoe was indeed a cipher. Like him, she seemed to have left that life behind, but what was she doing here at the end of the world? Even if, as rumor held, her husband's family had cast her off, what of her own family and acquaintance? Could she possibly be as entirely alone as appearances suggested? He shook his head thoughtfully. Something was not right here.

He pulled to the side of the road for a moment, to allow a cart to pass the other way. Caught up in his analysis of his new acquaintance, he almost failed to return the farmer's greeting. They exchanged a few civil words, but he could scarce have reported what they were, so distracted was he.

Venables had not entered Rosewood Cottage intending to examine it for clues to the owner's life; nonetheless, he had done so, and been disconcerted to find not the slightest hint of Mrs. Glencoe's past. There seemed to be no mementos, no memorabilia. No miniature of the husband in evidence. No regimental sword or sash.

Not even a twist of his hair in some frame or other, and she wore no locket. Though he saw no particular value in such displays, he knew about widows. He had often marked how, love or no, they raised what monuments they might as a way of affirming their station, despite the dusty imprint of death.

And just as there were no clues to the departed Captain Glencoe— so local gossip held his rank— neither were there signs by which one might read his widow. Venables knew the house had been purchased largely furnished, and remembered enough of the place to determine which pieces were the additions of the new owner. A few chairs, some framed lithographs of country scenes. There were books, but he had been unable to scan their titles. In short, anyone might live there.

The only thing which struck him as out of the ordinary were the several vases, overflowing with haphazard arrangements of bright flowers. Their transition from the garden to the drawing room had not transformed them into rigid arrangements, as was the custom in most houses.

Venables smiled as he thought of her reaction to his gift. He had been racking his brains trying to settle on a way to make an impression upon her— none of the artifices he had once used among ladies of the *ton* would do— when he came upon the motherless litter in a corner of the barn. Their little faces appealed to his heart, and he wondered if hers would be touched as well.

He had been entirely uncertain as to what he might expect from her when the basket's contents were revealed. But he had seen her transform from a staid widow to a delighted girl, almost as if she were a child who had dressed up in her mother's clothing, then grown tired of the game. It seemed as if the shadow he sensed in her had, for a moment, lifted, and allowed a shaft of sunshine to reach her heart. When he had departed, she was smiling still. Falstaff and Ophelia were curled up on her lap, while the third, an inky little fellow christened Prospero, nestled against her bosom.

Venables knew he had risked being tossed out on his ear for such effrontery, but his instincts had proved correct, and it had turned out well. She had invited him to call whenever he might have the leisure to see how the kittens got on— and that, after all, had been his sole aim.

He had been a little afraid she might view him merely in his official capacity, that their magic moment in the stone circle might, once she understood his role in the community, become nothing more than a relationship of doctor and patient. Her decision to have Maggie attend her when the time came was fortuitous. He was not of such a nature as to resent her preferring another in that capacity, and hopeful that it might allow their acquaintance to be more conventional. She would be far more likely now to see him in light of . . . well, a man.

Perhaps the time had come, he mused. Perhaps, after all, Heaven might forgive and allow him to be happy.

Alden Venables arrived at his own gate, almost without knowing it. His mind had been so occupied, the landscape had slipped by him, the turns taken automatically.

"Ah, doctor, you are come home then, are you?"

The doctor set his bag in the entry and greeted his housekeeper, Mrs. Maiden. "There's lamb pie for supper," she said, wiping her floury hands upon her apron, "but before you eat, you must first turn about and call at the Wallers'."

"Is something amiss there?" he asked. "All seemed well when I saw them yesterday."

"Naught but a simple mishap," she told him. " 'Tis to be hoped the reverend has merely given his ankle a twist, not broken it, as his wife thinks. Mrs. Waller begs you will have a look, and I told her you would."

He nodded, not unused to the woman's pledging his time without leave. He was here to serve, after all, not to indulge himself.

"And if you would be so kind," the woman went on crisply, "take Charlie and George away with you. All day they've been wicked enough to make the angels weep, and that's a fact."

He sighed and shook his head ruefully. Some of his projects took longer to show progress than others. "What have the little criminals been up to now?" he asked.

"The question is more," she returned with a long-suffering sigh, "what have they *not* been up to?"

Alden allowed himself a heartfelt groan. "Ought I to sit down," he asked, "or do I dare face the tidings standing?"

"I hope I've no need to remind you, doctor," she returned tartly, " 'tis you brought the savages here. You must listen to the tales without support." She took a deep breath and began counting on her fingers.

"First, they terrified Lucy into a fit with a snake, so that she could not help me prepare your supper. Next, they set the dogs to chase a badger through the kitchen, upsetting a tray of tarts I was saving for your tea tomorrow. The dogs then worried themselves to fits over whether to eat the tarts or follow the badger, all the time those boys laughing as if they would break apart. Then the rascals got into the cream as was setting up, ate it all, and did not even have the Christian decency to be sick afterward! I do not suppose I could persuade you to put them to bed with a dose of laudanum?"

"I suggest we hoard it for ourselves, Mrs. Maiden," he laughed. "And the little newcomers? How do they fare?"

Mrs. Maiden bit her lower lip thoughtfully. "Well enough. They are very quiet, though," she said. "Too quiet for children, if you ask me. I do not think they said more than ten words between them today. But perhaps that can be laid at the door of those two rapscallions as have plagued me today. I could not blame the dear little girls for being shocked to silence at such naughtiness. Charlie and George, indeed! They ought better to have been called Imp and Scratch!''

"Very likely, my dear Mrs. Maiden," he agreed. "Indeed you are a paragon to have braved their mischief. Do not fear. I shall take the pair of them along with me to the Wallers', and you will have some respite. I warn you, however, if those good souls have cause to regret my impetuosity, I must lay the blame at your door."

"For a few moments' peace, I will take that risk. And what is more," she added darkly, "if the two of them should be misplaced somewhere along the road, you would not hear me complain."

"I thank you for your forbearance, Mrs. Maiden," he said as he lifted his bag once more. "Anyone else would have sold them to the gypsies."

"Do not imagine it is my virtue that I have not done so, doctor. There are simply no gypsies to be had!"

"Thank you for coming, Dr. Venables." Mrs. Waller arose as he entered the parlor, where the reverend was resting with his foot well elevated.

"You may reclaim your thanks when you find I have not arrived unaccompanied," he told her.

"Not another— ?" she began.

"Never fear," he laughed. "Nothing so dire as another four-legged addition to your household, but Christian charity demands I be forthright. Mrs. Maiden has banished Charlie and George from her sight for the present, so I have sent them off to the barn to assist your Haggerty, until I am finished here."

Although his wife looked somewhat alarmed, the reverend smiled wanly. "An excellent notion," he said. "Haggerty will at least have the presence of mind to clap the little demons in irons, should they play at setting the place afire. Tell me, doctor, do you never bring *angels* home from your travels?"

He shook his head. "Not so often as I would like. You must know it is exceedingly rare for angels to be abandoned to the streets— with imps and injured animals it is otherwise, I fear. I have a pair of little girls, though, who *appear* angelic enough."

"So did Charlie and George," Mrs. Waller reminded him, "before they became used to wholesome meals and your easy ways."

"That is too true," he sighed. "Perhaps, however, we can with our combined efforts keep this villainous pair from the noose until they achieve the ripe age of ten."

"Perhaps," the reverend allowed, rather tentatively, it seemed to Venables, "but let me tell you here and now, that I draw the line at preparing them for the ministry!"

"Heaven forfend!" Mrs. Waller exclaimed.

"Indeed!" the doctor smiled as he made his way to his patient's side. "Although my heart forewarns me that the role of sexton might appeal to them enormously."

"Ringing bells and digging graves!" Mrs. Waller laughed, shaking her head. "I can see it all too clearly. Give us your word you will not inform them such occupations exist!"

"You have my word as a gentleman," the doctor promised. "Now tell me, Reverend. How did this sorry mishap came about? Confess— you have been swinging from trees, have you not?"

"So you have discovered my secret vice, doctor!" He shook his head ruefully as he went on, "No, I must confess it was nothing so daring. It is merely that I did not watch my step, while on my afternoon ramble."

"It is difficult to always be aware of one's surroundings," his wife added with tart good humor, "when one has his nose in a book during that ramble. Doctor, you must warn my husband of the dangers of mixing intellectual and physical pursuits!"

Dr. Venables examined the swollen extremity before him. "I should think," he commented, "that ample warning had already been issued!"

"And a penalty exacted," the reverend added, paling as the doctor gently rotated the injured ankle. "How long until I am mended, do you think?"

"That depends on you as much as nature," Venables told him. "If you rest and allow healing, as little as two weeks. Otherwise, a good deal longer. No bones have been broken, but the muscles and tendons have suffered a good deal. You must stay off it at all accounts. Is there someone you can call upon to assist you in your duties here?"

"I suppose," the reverend said thoughtfully, "I might request Reverend Burne in Plymouth to send his curate to me. But then I should have to suffer his company— he talks when he should listen. I had rather bear the pain, if you must know."

The doctor nodded. "Have you a cane?"

"There are several from Uncle Erasmus's time," Mrs. Waller said. Then she laughed. "How ironic, Enos, that it should come to this so soon!"

"It is my punishment," he said ruefully, "for my foolish mockery as a youth."

Venables looked at him quizzically.

"Yes," his wife explained, "however serious he now seems, Enos was once quite a scamp. Had you told me as a child I would end by marrying my cousin, I should have called you a base liar! He was ever imitating his elders, when the opportunity arose. Uncle Erasmus caught him at it once, hobbling about on a cane and quoting dire passages from Scripture."

"What's more, I was using one of those self-same canes which I must now use to good purpose! Perhaps," he went on thoughtfully, "I might use this mischance as an illustration in my next sermon. What think you, doctor? No sin, however small, goes unpunished?"

Venables began to wrap the reverend's ankle slowly, and it was a moment before he answered. "That depends," he said at last, "on how you wish your parishioners to view the Almighty— a merciful father or a heartless judge."

"Yes, that thorny problem again— will it be Old Testament or New?"

When Mrs. Waller escorted Venables to the door after he had finished with her husband, she asked, "How did you find Mrs. Glencoe this afternoon?"

Although he was good friends with both the reverend and his wife, something— perhaps a superstitious fear of losing the happiness he seemed to have discovered— made him reluctant to reveal his interest in the widow. "It is as she said yesterday," he replied briefly. "She does well enough."

Mrs. Waller nodded. "I do not mean to pry, of course, but I have been a little worried about her."

"It is little wonder you should be— a lady alone, facing the birth of a child."

"It is not," she went on slowly, "her . . . condition so much that prompts my concern. It is her spirit. Oh, I know you will say, well, she is after all a recent widow, but I fear that has little to do with the . . . well, for want of a better word, the *darkness* I have sensed about her."

So he was not alone in his assessment. He said nothing, though, and merely nodded for Mrs. Waller to proceed.

"In some ways, I have been where she is," she

said softly. "I have not confided this in many, but once— before I married Enos— I was engaged to another man whom I loved very much. He died."

The doctor put a hand on her shoulder. She shook her head. "I did my best to recover, but it would not do. I was grateful when my cousin offered for me, and we have built a pleasant life together, but I have never expunged my grief— merely assimilated it into the rest of my life, like poor Annie with her crooked leg. I go about living, doing what I must, even laughing when I may, but I am still aware of his absence. With Mrs. Glencoe, though, it is different."

Venables frowned. "How do you mean?"

She took a moment before proceeding, choosing her words carefully. "It is as if . . . as if her heart has never sung. Only the mention of her baby brings joy to her eyes, and then it is guarded, as if this treasure, too, might be snatched away."

They passed into the garden together, both lost in thought. The sage lady read people very well, it seemed. She had given words to his nebulous awareness that something aside from the obvious was amiss in Mrs. Glencoe's life. What, he wondered, did Mrs. Waller make of him and his oddities? Gathering broken children, even animals, during his travels and bringing them here. Could she divine the memories that drove *him*?

"I have been thinking," Mrs. Waller continued, "that it would be a very good thing if her heart were to be lightened before her child arrived . . . and that you and she might between you lighten your burdens."

He looked at her sharply. What could she mean? Were his emotions that transparent then? And what might she know of his burdens?

"You have returned with new protégés, I understand," she went on. "Might they be of a nature to be companions to Mrs. Glencoe? Is there aught she could teach them?"

"You are a redoubtable woman, Mrs. Waller," he said, a good deal relieved. "Perhaps you have hit on the very thing. The little girls I brought back with me are six and eight. They are very quiet— I do not know if they have even learned their letters. Quite likely not, considering the surroundings from which they came. They are orphans, and lived with an old woman who sent them daily into the streets to pick rags."

"Poor little souls," she murmured.

"Not forever," he assured her. "They do smile quite readily now that they are in the country, so I have begun to hold out a great deal of hope for them."

Just then they were interrupted by the sudden appearance of two urchins, their clothes badly torn and faces painted with a suspicious innocence. "Charlie and George!" the doctor said, shaking his head wearily. "As for these two I can make no such predictions. Come now," he said, addressing the pair, "what have the two of you been up to?"

Both boys erupted into a flurry of self-righteous explanations, each attempting to out-do the other in volume and velocity.

"Enough," Venables ordered, taking them each by the collar and physically separating them. "One at a time. Come now, George?"

" 'Twas Charlie's wicked idea, it was," the child began defensively.

" 'E's flammin' you!" the other interrupted with loud indignation. " 'Twas him thought of it, and it's him 'as got the rent in his britches to prove it!"

"And whose fault might that be, I ask you?" George scoffed. " 'Twas you, not me, thought of the goat to begin with— "

"Perhaps I am better off not knowing what went on," the doctor muttered.

"Then we'll not plague you with explanations," Charlie offered generously. "Just leave it alone then, right and tight."

"However, I dare not!" The doctor looked apologetically at Mrs. Waller who, despite the alarm in her eyes, seemed to be hiding a smile behind her handkerchief. "Ah, here is poor Mr. Haggerty, looking like a thunder cloud. Perhaps he can illuminate us."

The said Mr. Haggerty was rubbing his forehead, where a lump was now rising. When the doctor came forward to examine the injury, however, he shook his head, saying, " 'Tis naught wrong with me but a bump, and, beggin' your pardons, I'd rather a sore head than a sore arse, like yon knave." Here, he jerked his head at

George. "Next time, p'raps they'll be wiser and not try their luck at milking a billy goat."

Venables felt the corner of his mouth twitch. It would never do for the boys to observe his amusement. Schooling his expression, he commanded them, on pain of his severe wrath, to sit quietly in the curricle and behave themselves. Abashed, he turned to Mrs. Waller. "I pray Mrs. Glencoe does not hear rumors of my charges' comportment, else I shall never persuade her to consider taking the little girls under her tutelage."

"Should that occur, I happen to know a sure way to her heart," Mrs. Waller said.

He raised his brows at her in inquiry.

"Curry," the lady said succinctly.

"Curry?"

She nodded mysteriously. "Consider it a form of rampion."

Eight

. . . *So, you see, my dear Olivia,* Marianne wrote, *you must not fear my falling prey to boredom. Between the intriguing pronouncements of Old Maggie and the antics of little Falstaff, Ophelia, and Prospero, I haven't a moment to pine for what I have left behind— except for your company, dearest one. That is not so easily replaced. Still, I must . . .*

"Beg pardon, Mrs. Glencoe," Annie interrupted.

Marianne set her pen aside. "What is it?" she asked, smiling. "Never tell me that fat Falstaff has discovered the pantry?"

"Nothing so dreadful as that," the maid returned. "It is just Dr. Venables has arrived, calling to see if you are at leisure."

"If I never am anymore," she returned, "he may blame those naughty kittens. My poor sister will have to read my letter through their little paw prints." She smiled as she glanced at the basket where they were, for once, all curled together in repose. "The doctor seems to have made quite a favorite of you, Annie. Have you been long acquainted with him?"

"Ever so long, Missus. Since I was a child. He's

ever so good to me, for besides looking after my poor limb, he has even set up a dowry for me, when the time comes." The girl's face glowed when she spoke of the doctor. Such interest seemed unprecedented unless . . . no, surely he was too young to be the girl's father. Yet what else would explain this sort of attention? Venables was kind at heart, of course, but still . . .

"Show him in, Annie," she said, "but tell him plain he must check any four-legged creatures at the door!"

When the doctor entered, he was smiling broadly, and, she noted with some dismay, bearing yet another covered basket.

"What is this? Have you brought me more orphans?" she asked incredulously.

He smiled in response, the corners of his mouth twitching in a manner which reminded her of a child bent on mischief. "Now then, it is merely a small tribute," he answered mysteriously.

Marianne felt her heart soar, then plunge, at this further evidence of the doctor's attention. At once, her emotions put her on her guard. Be careful, she told herself. You must be careful. There is no good to come of such foolish romantical notions. She glanced down at her rapidly growing middle, summoning reason. Surely a gentleman could feel no interest in one so matronly as she had become. Surely he was merely fulfilling Mrs. Waller's prediction: her help was to be enlisted in more than the raising of kittens. Perhaps he would ask her to sew for the poor heathens of India, or read improving books to housebound invalids.

"So you have spirited the crown jewels here to Cornwall, have you?" she asked archly, lowering herself carefully into a chair.

"You injure me, Mrs. Glencoe," he exclaimed. "I have brought something even more rare."

As she raised her eyebrows in question, he set the basket in her lap and said, "Sniff."

As she did so, she felt her mouth immediately begin to water. "Curry!" she cried. "Doctor, you are unfair! What sort of friend is our Mrs. Waller to reveal my secret passion?"

"Do not forget," he laughed, "that the friendship between Mrs. Waller and myself holds claim to a far older acquaintance."

"And what of the bond between women?" She shook her head. "What a fix I am in now!"

She pulled the napkin from the basket. "Oh! It smells heavenly! Whatever will be my forfeit?"

"Do not worry, Mrs. Glencoe. It is enough to see that my poor efforts have pleased you. However, if you should feel inclined to humor me in my request, I should not take it amiss."

"And what is this . . . request?" she asked, glancing longingly at the spicy dish of meat.

"It is merely . . ." he began. Then he frowned. "Perhaps you should eat first. Here, let me ring for Annie to bring you a tray and some cutlery."

Appetite warred with good sense, but at last she nodded, and in a few minutes she was savoring the exotic concoction. "You are indeed a jewel among men, doctor," she sighed. It was true. Jewels and trinkets she knew well enough how to disregard, but kittens and curry? She had no notion how such gifts were to be esteemed, or what they might require by way of response. Just then, a round ball of fur pounced upon her lap and a pink nose sniffed delicately in the direction of her plate.

"Oh, no! Not so fast, little Falstaff," she cried, picking the fellow up and handing him to her companion. "I shall indulge your appetite in all other ways, but this is *my* nuncheon! Besides, I do not think such a dish would suit your constitution."

"Not in the least," the doctor concurred, settling the kitten on his lap and stroking him under the chin. "I say, he certainly seems to be thriving here. It has been no more than four days, but I wager he has almost doubled in size. How do the others fare?"

She laughed. "They look like fat caterpillars. See, they are there by the fireplace. To think I was worried about Ophelia!"

He glanced at the basket. "I would not have guessed. They will soon be big enough to eat unassisted." He raised the kitten he held up to his face. "I fear this one will be demanding his own dish of pudding and a syllabub twice a day."

Marianne grimaced at the thought. The very notion of some foods prompted a shudder of revulsion. She wiped her mouth and rang for Annie to clear away the dishes. "Let us take a turn in the garden, doctor, and you may argue your case."

"As it happens," he replied, "that is the very place to do so."

She took his arm as they entered the garden, and he led her along the path, stopping here and there to admire the remaining blooms. Despite the notion that he was about to present a case which might lead to disruption of her quiet life, Marianne found she felt altogether comfortable as they approached the subject. It must be that, whatever he would eventually ask of her, it would not be accompanied by the worldly bartering which had in the past assailed her spirit.

"I must tell you, there are intruders in your garden," he said softly.

She looked at him narrowly. "Whatever do you mean, doctor?"

He placed a finger against his lips and silently nodded to a stand of greenery in the distance. Under a canopy of golden leaves, knelt two little girls plucking daisies. She drew in her breath sharply. Russet-haired, one with sparkling blue eyes, the other with green. They were as sweet-faced as a pair of kittens.

"Who are they?" she whispered, reluctant to disturb their pastime.

"I am afraid I know little more than their names and a bit of their recent past," he told her in a low voice. "They are called Jane and Becky— Becky is the smaller of the two— and I found them a fortnight ago on the streets of Edinburgh. Becky had fallen, weak from hunger as it turns out. As I rounded a corner, I was fortunate enough to spy Jane pulling her from the path of horses. I took them up with me and discovered they were employed— enslaved rather— by an old reprobate they called Old Peg, who sent them out each day to pick rags. Should they have survived their childhood, I am sure she would have sold them for other purposes."

She drew in her breath. "But they are mere babies," she whispered.

The doctor nodded, but said nothing more. Marianne shuddered as she watched them, now engaged in their innocent play. She had judged her own life wretched, but she had never fully lost control of her fate. Its direction might have been diverted by the intolerant constraints of society, but she had always retained some power. "Is the world full of naught but monsters?" she asked hollowly.

"There are times it would seem so," he replied shortly. "In any case, this is the favor I would ask of you: Take them when you may, draw them out, try to teach them gentle ways?"

Marianne felt the full force of this compliment, and her heart warmed to him despite her judgment's warnings. For all she had felt her life useless in the past, she realized there were things she could teach the little girls, and perhaps help build the foundation of a better life. "Let me meet them first," she said slowly, "and see how they take to me. If we get on, I shall do what I can."

"That sounds like a wise proposition. Thank

you, Mrs. Glencoe." He caught her hand and pressed it for a moment, then led her to where the girls sat.

"Jane, Becky," he began. The little girls looked up at him, but their eyes, when they flitted to Marianne, were veiled with caution. "This is my good friend, Mrs. Glencoe, of whom I told you. Do you remember how to make your curtsies?"

They stood, exchanged a silent glance, and each traced a wobbly little bob in Marianne's direction. Jane, apparently the older of the two, smoothed her pinafore and whispered, "Good day, Missus," in a soft brogue.

"Good day to you, Jane. And good day, Becky," Marianne said gently. "Would you like to step into my house for a bit of tea? I believe there may be some cherry tarts for you there."

Again the girls glanced silently at one another, then at the doctor. He nodded to them. "I think that would be a capital idea. I happen to know that Mrs. Glencoe's cook makes the finest tarts in three counties— although I beg you will not tell Mrs. Maiden that I told you so."

The girls still looked somewhat unsure. Marianne stooped to their level and whispered, "I've three fine kittens, too, who are longing to be played with."

Jane frowned, then said, "Auld Peg says kittens be evil, and wouldna let us hae none of 'em." The child pursed her lips for a moment, then went on thoughtfully, "But I say then kittens must be kind and good, for Auld Peg was a liar."

Marianne held out her hands to them, and the foursome went into the house together. There, the girls took in their surroundings with wide eyes. Marianne rang for Annie and told her, ''We shall need a very special tea for my guests— we shall need lots of cream and tarts and anything else Mrs. Bridges thinks would be welcome.''

Annie grinned at the little girls and returned a short time later with a heavily laden tray. When she did so, their eyes went wide and their mouths made little O's. Jane ventured a slight smile in Marianne's direction, and Dr. Venables prepared a plate for each of them.

Marianne was still quite full from having eaten the curry such a short time earlier, but it did her heart good to watch the little girls avail themselves of the treats. She even allowed them to take the kittens onto their laps and lick cream from the girls' little fingers. Though their actions, and the joy they seemed to receive as a result, seemed all that was young and innocent, Marianne could not help but notice that the girls' eyes were somehow old beyond their years.

Then it struck her. That was what linked her and the doctor, and now these little ones. Beyond a serene and sometimes playful front, there lingered the shadow of pain. She knew well enough in her own case what lay behind this darkness. The story of the little girls explained theirs. But the doctor? What secrets lay behind that lively smile, in the depths of those sometimes sad eyes? Perhaps she would never know.

Nine

Olivia, Lady Blakensly, stared pensively into the fire. Although it was her favorite hour of the day, when the children were brought to her before Nurse took them up to bed, their cheerful prattle drifted by her, as if it were no more than the distant sound of footsteps in the passage or muted clinking of glassware on the sideboard.

"You are looking rather pulled, my love," her husband told her as he seated himself at her side and gently took her hand in his. "Is anything amiss? I hope you are not unwell?"

She shook her head and summoned a smile. "Not in the least, William—merely a bit distracted today."

"I see you have had a letter," he remarked.

She glanced at the table where the missive sat. In her perplexity, she had folded it into small squares and unfolded it again, so that it was now as crumpled as an autumn leaf. Without a word, she handed it to her husband. As he perused it, she beckoned the children to her, kissed each on the tops of their curly heads, and sent them away to the nursery.

Lord Blakensly, when he had finished his perusal, said nothing, merely replaced the letter on the table and took his wife into his arms. She leaned her head against his shoulder and sighed.

"It does not seem right," she murmured, "that I should have so much, and my dear Marianne must scratch to find a bit of happiness."

Nor was it right, Lord Blakensly reflected. He knew several among the members of his club who had debauched their way through their youths. They were now accepted in the best of homes. Men could repair their reputations in this world. Women, unfortunately, could not.

"Your sister sounds quite content in her letter," he said. "But you, of course, know her well enough to read beyond mere words."

"That is just it!" Olivia pulled herself from him and paced to the window. "Gardens and eccentric herb women and orphaned kittens, indeed! Oh, how she struggles to sound content for my sake. She is all alone," she fretted, "facing a first childbirth among strangers. How I wish I could go to her."

"I wish indeed you might," returned her husband, "and you know well I should not forbid it, Olivia, were it not for your own delicate condition."

She turned away from him and continued to look out onto the street, clutching her arms about her in a way which made her look like a forlorn little sparrow. This was not his gay Olivia at all.

Blakensly poured himself a brandy, feeling altogether helpless in the face of his wife's wretchedness. Even though she had borne their two elder children with apparent ease and in excellent health, he did not think she was having quite such an easy time with this one. She looked quite pinched about the eyes, frailer than he ever remembered, and he blamed it on her sister.

"What possessed her to go so far away from me?" Olivia whispered. "Why did I not do more to stop her?"

He came behind her and placed his hands on her shoulders. "I believe your sister knows her own mind. You did what you could to persuade her otherwise, and to no avail."

"If only she had confided her difficulty to Cheswick. I am persuaded he would never have let her go away in that mad fashion."

"Come now. You know quite well he must have done so—there could have been no other choice for him, given his marriage." He rocked her in his arms a moment. "Calm yourself, Olivia. Your sister has merely written to tell you she is well and happy."

"Of course, she must reassure me as to her circumstances. What she *tells* me is unexceptionable." Olivia shook her head disconsolately. "But it was ever her nature to keep me at a distance, wrapped in cotton wool, so naturally I conjure up all sorts of unpleasant pictures of what she does not tell me. If only I knew for certain she were truly well, I could rest much easier."

"Do not work yourself into a sick headache," he said, kissing her temple. "Remember, you must obey your husband, and I forbid you to be unwell."

She leaned into his arms and rested her head upon his shoulder. "If only I might know," she whispered.

Later that evening, Lord Blakensly found his way to his club. Unlike many of his companions, he repaired there rather less often after his marriage than before it. Olivia had retired early, however, and, distracted as he was by his wife's concerns, he found himself poor company. He needed to think what to do. He pitied his sister-in-law, but he could not allow her plight to distress his wife so powerfully.

He settled himself in a deep leather chair and asked the attendant to bring him some brandy. There were few others about; doubtless his fellow members were occupying themselves in a more entertaining manner this early in the evening. He picked up a paper and glanced at the account of yesterday's debate in the House of Lords. His own name was mentioned briefly, he noted with a faint rush of pride. He must remember to show the item to Olivia.

"Good evening, Blakensly."

He glanced up and frowned. Monte Cheswick also found refuge in the club tonight. He had quite forgot the young man was a member, and it rankled to see the other's smiling face, oblivious to all the harm he had wrought.

"Cheswick," he returned tersely. He turned once again to the paper.

Cheswick stood awkwardly a moment, then drew a chair beside him, and sat down. "Forgive me for intruding on you, but I must tell you how much I admired your speech last week. It expressed my sentiments exactly."

Blakensly nodded, but said nothing. Cheswick looked disconcerted, but forged on, "I must ask you something. I do not know quite how to phrase it . . . but you must tell me. Have I done aught to offend you?"

Cheswick's earnest face awaited his answer, but it was a moment before Blakensly offered one. "You do not, perhaps, know," he said quietly, "that Marianne Gardiner is my wife's sister."

Cheswick sat back in his chair, looking as if he had been struck. Taking pity, Blakensly poured a measure of brandy and offered it to the young man before him. Cheswick took the glass, but did not drink.

"No," he said softly. "I did not know." The sound of a clock ticking underscored the silence which fell between them.

"I don't believe I ever had an idea of Marianne's family," Cheswick went on in a hollow voice. "I had heard she was of our circle, or had been at one time, but I never asked . . . I merely took."

"You are not the first man to have entered such an arrangement before his marriage," Lord Blakensly murmured. "It is something our sex takes entirely too much for granted, I am afraid. Indeed, I think I should have spent the rest of my life behind the blinders of tradition, had I not fallen in love with Olivia. Had I not heard her sister's story from one who loved her."

"Marianne— have you heard aught of her?" Cheswick asked wretchedly.

"My wife has had a letter." Cheswick looked at him expectantly. "I understand she seems . . . well."

"There is something more, isn't there? I know she is not in London, for I tried to call and they told me at her house she has been gone these three months."

"It is true. She is no longer in London."

Cheswick frowned as he swirled the brandy in his glass. "So, to whom has she gone now?"

"It is not," he said tersely," a matter of *whom*." Blakensly deliberated a moment. In his heart, he felt that, though he had made no promise to keep her sister's whereabouts secret, his wife's word bound him as well. He knew, however, that Olivia regretted her pledge, and that Cheswick's ignorance of the situation, the news of his paying marriage calls about London with his new wife, wounded her.

"First, I must ask you as a gentleman to act with prudence in regard to this matter."

Cheswick leaned forward. "You have my word."

Blakensly glanced at the foyer. Other members were beginning to arrive. "Then come, let us find someplace where we may be more private."

Sir Frederick Stratford reclined on a sofa facing a comfortable fire in a quiet room at his club. It was a good thing he had kept up his dues, he reflected, for it was impossible to return to his rooms, where a variety of bad-tempered creditors awaited him. The club offered solace in the form of meals, brandy, and the occasional card game, until he could raise enough funds to seek refuge back on the Continent. True, his luck had been abysmal lately, but that was a sure sign it was about to turn.

Just then he heard the door open, and frowned as it closed again and he heard a voice say, "This shall do well enough, I imagine."

Two pairs of footsteps crossed the room in the direction of the window. With any luck, the intruders did not mean to stay, and he would not have to trouble himself to either reveal himself or move from his comfortable position.

"What is it, Blakensly?"

He recognized the speaker's voice immediately as young Monte Cheswick. And the other was apparently Lord Blakensly. What could this pair discuss that was of a private nature? Stratford smiled and shifted his position slightly that he might better hear. Knowledge was power.

"My wife is considerably distressed, and though she has pledged herself to secrecy, I think it my duty to inform you that her sister is carrying your child."

"Marianne is— ?" Cheswick's voice sounded like the dull click of an unloaded gun.

"Yes. My wife is . . . in a delicate way herself, and I believe it would relieve her mind to know that this matter has been brought to your attention. I trust you will do all in your power to see that Marianne and the child are provided for."

Little wheels began to turn in Stratford's mind. It was a very good thing the British were so squeamish about these matters, he mused. He had found it otherwise on his visits to the Continent, but at home, such secrets were so much easier to turn to his benefit.

"Of course, of course . . ." Cheswick said hurriedly. "To think, I had not the least clue. Where is Marianne?"

There was a pause and a rustle of paper.

"Here is her direction. I shall trust you to be circumspect."

"Cornwall!" Cheswick released a low sigh. "I had thought I might be able to visit, to at least see for myself— "

"I believe it would be best for all concerned," Blakensly interrupted, not unkindly, "if you did not. There is little to be accomplished by doing such a thing. Send her assistance by one whom you can trust, and fix your attention on your own concerns."

There was silence for a moment, then one set of footsteps crossed the room, and the door could be heard to open and close. Stratford smiled. Luck, it seemed, had returned even sooner than he imagined it would. Where there was scandal, there was money. And Marianne. He should like very much to repay her for her haughtiness— as if she thought she were too good for the likes of him. He would have her at his mercy before long, like a pretty butterfly firmly fixed in a spider's web.

He pulled himself up quietly and observed that Cheswick was standing motionless, looking out the window onto the street, his sunken posture the very vision of nauseous remorse. Stratford cleared his throat, and Cheswick spun about.

"You must forgive me, my dear Cheswick," he smiled. "I had been dozing over there and did not realize I was privy to a confidential conversation."

Color flooded the younger man's countenance. "Of all the— you might have said something to make yourself known," he cried hotly.

"Do not fret, my friend," Stratford said smoothly. "Your little secret will be safe with me. Indeed, I am every bit as distressed as you to hear this news. Do not forget, I am also a devotee of our dear Miss Gardiner. Trust me, I should not for anything repeat a single word of what I have just heard."

"For *that* much, I thank you," Cheswick spat.

Anger was good, Stratford reflected. It made fools of even the wise, and young Cheswick could hardly be counted among that number. "What do you intend to do?" he asked.

Cheswick said nothing, but turned once again to the window.

"What a predicament," Stratford went on quietly. "Something must be done for our poor Marianne. And yet . . . and yet there is your wife, is there not?"

"Yes," Cheswick said evenly. "There is my wife."

"I understand she keeps you on a rather short lead, or have I heard amiss?"

Cheswick turned on his heel and regarded him with narrowed eyes.

"I do not mean to offend you, my friend. I merely acknowledge your difficulty."

"Yes, my *difficulty.*"

Stratford extricated a delicate snuffbox, took a pinch, and sneezed into his handkerchief. "I think, however, I may be able to help you out. Unlike you, I may come and go as I please. It would not be difficult for me to serve as— how would you say?— a go-between. I could go to her, ascertain what she might need, and perhaps set your mind at rest."

Cheswick appeared to deliberate, then nodded. "Inspite of my *short lead,* as you so aptly phrase it, I do have some resources. I will do all within my power for Marianne."

Crossing to a table, he availed himself of writing materials and scribbled a few lines. "This empowers my man of business to put £500 at your disposal. That should be sufficient for the present."

"Yes," Stratford concurred, taking the paper

from him and placing it in his waistcoat pocket, "for the present. Now will you join me in a glass of brandy? You look in need of a restorative. My dear friend," he said, looking at the other narrowly, "I hope your pallor does not suggest you fancy yourself in love with the woman."

Cheswick shook his head. "No," he whispered. "Merely nostalgic for a remembered happiness."

"That is well," Stratford told him. "You must be honest with yourself. Marianne Gardiner is a beautiful woman and a pleasant companion, but she is, after all, a whore."

The older gentleman took a step backward as Cheswick's hands clenched into fists. "It is for your own good that I tell you this: the brat could as well be mine, or that of some half-dozen others. Come now, you could not expect faithfulness in a woman of that stamp?"

Cheswick did not answer. Stratford made as if to put his arm about the younger man's shoulder, but his gesture met with icy rejection. "Do not give this matter another thought," Stratford said. "I shall add my contribution to yours. And, if necessary, I shall let you know when more funds are needed. Other than that, you need not be bothered with this matter again."

Ten

Marianne sat before a blazing fire, Jane and Becky nestled on either side of her, and the kittens, sleeping for once, in a basket at her feet. The fair weather had finally forsaken them, but though the wind whistled round the corners of Rosewood Cottage, all was snug within.

". . . x, y, and zed," Jane pronounced slowly from the little book before her.

"Very good," Marianne smiled. "You and Becky must practice during the week to come, and then I will show you how all of these letters are put together into words and stories."

Jane sighed and looked up at her soulfully. "Must we be waitin' till next time for a story?"

Marianne smiled. "I have sent for some story books," she explained, "but they have not arrived yet. Perhaps, however, I can remember one from my nursery days."

"A story right out of your own head?" Jane asked, her eyes wide.

"Yes, right out of my own head— we will hope it does not suffer in the translation."

How quickly these two had taken to her, trusted her— rather like the kittens, she realized.

Dr. Venables had begun by bringing them by
with him when he had finished his daily calls,
then, when they had grown comfortable enough,
encouraged them to find their way to the cottage
on their own. Becky was still very quiet, speaking in a whispered undertone, if at all. Jane,
however, made up for her little sister's silence,
chatting companionably like an old friend. At
odd moments, Marianne could still discern the
remnants of the child's initial watchfulness, but
she gave it little thought. Perhaps in this life,
such caution was a good thing, for who knew
when it might provide a necessary lens to view
a wicked world?

Before beginning her story, Marianne poured
out another cup of chocolate for the children,
just as Annie entered. "You've more callers,
ma'am," the maid told her with a frown, "though
these last may not be so welcome as the first."

Raising her eyebrows, Marianne glanced past
Annie to see two grimy faces peeking past her
skirts. Charlie and George, was it? She had
glimpsed them once, but had heard innumer-
able tales of their naughtiness. She hoped their
visit did not portend a parade of hedgehogs
through her parlor, or a polecat in the barn.
From her side came Jane's whispered pronouncement, "Wicked boys! Please, Missus,
dinna let them spoil our story."

Marianne sympathized, remembering the an-
tipathy of little girls for those of the opposite
gender, but, watching the boys gaze longingly

at the well-laden tea tray, she found she had not
the heart to turn them away.

"Good afternoon," she said. "You may come
in, but we are just about to have a story, so you
must sit very still and listen quietly, if you are
to stay."

The boys exchanged a glance and seated
themselves on the floor near the kittens. George
advanced a tentative hand to pet one of them,
but Jane immediately hissed, "Dinna touch
'em," and he withdrew it. Marianne bit her
tongue to keep from smiling. Apparently, Jane
commanded respect.

As the girls snuggled closer, Marianne took a
deep breath. "Once upon a time, there lived a
princess."

"Was she beautiful?" Jane asked.

"Why yes, of course. She was so beautiful that
songs were written about her, and artists begged
for the honor of painting her portrait."

"But our princess in London been't beautiful,
you know," Jane informed her. "Dr. Venables
showed a picture of her to me 'n' Becky, and
she looks like a sad cow, right enow."

Marianne could hardly deny the truth of this
assessment, but thought it best to make no comment. "Well," she went on quickly, "*this* princess
was very beautiful. She had rich red hair, and
green eyes that turned up at the corners, just
like a kitten's."

Beside her, Becky, who was endowed with just
such hair and eyes, giggled. Progress. "One day,
she was walking through the woods picking flow-

ers, when she came upon a handsome young man."

"And he was good and kind," Jane pronounced.

"Why, how do you know?" Marianne asked.

"Handsome young men are *always* good and kind," the child averred.

Marianne winced. It was not *always* so, as experience had taught her. "Well, this one was not!" she improvised. "In fact, he was the wickedest young man in the world, for all he was so handsome."

"Aweel! What sort of wickedness did he do?" Jane asked eagerly.

"Aye!" Charlie broke in. "Was he a murderer?"

Marianne frowned. This story was becoming more difficult to tell than she had anticipated, and far from the simple tale she had initially embarked upon. "No, he wasn't a murderer yet," she told them, "but he did kick his horse every day and stole cherry tarts from children."

Jane nodded. "That is right wicked. But did he love kittens?"

"No. In fact, he particularly disliked them."

"Prob'ly he set dogs upon 'em," George put in.

"Wicked, wicked," Jane sighed.

"Yes, he was," Marianne continued, "and when he saw the lovely princess, he decided immediately he would have her as his own. At first, the princess was blinded by his fair face and thought him an honest young man. But one day, she saw him beat his servant, and decided to have nothing more to do with him."

Now what? She searched her mind for something to add to the tale, something that would set it back in the direction she had first intended.

"The end?" asked George quizzically after a moment's silence.

"Certainly not," Marianne said, suddenly inspired. "The princess decided that the young man should be taught a lesson. She called upon her good fairy godmother to ask for some advice, and between the two of them they devised a plan—"

"I know! I know!" Jane interrupted, bouncing up and down. "They turned him into a poor horse, and he were made to pull wagons through town."

It was not what Marianne had thought to say herself, but it seemed quite fitting. "What a bright little thing you are! That was the very thing. They treated him kindly, though, and did not make him work very hard, and at the end of three years, the fairy allowed him to—"

"No."

It was little Becky who had spoken. Fascinated by this sudden outburst, Marianne saw that the little girl's jaw was now set quite stubbornly. "No," the child repeated in a low whisper. "The bad man stayed a horse the rest of his days, and the children was allowed to ride him up and down the town."

Becky's tone brooked no contradiction, nor

did Marianne wish to interfere with the child's newly found tongue. "Very well," she nodded. "I can see you have heard the tale told another way."

"Did the princess ever marry?" Jane asked.

"She did one day," Marianne said. "She married a very nice young prince, who was not nearly so handsome as the first, but who allowed her to keep as many kittens as she wanted in the palace."

Jane helped herself to another tart. *"That* was a lovely story, to be sure, Missus. And will the books have others like it?"

"Not precisely," she smiled, "but I am certain we shall like some of them quite well."

"Did that princess ever have babies?" Jane asked.

"Oh, yes. All princesses, each one lovelier and happier than the next."

Jane looked up at Marianne, then glanced down at her middle. "Are you growin' a baby?"

The boys leaned forward curiously, prompting a sudden blush of self-consciousness. Still, Marianne allowed herself a laugh. Such a question from any other quarter would have unnerved her altogether, but the children's innocent curiosity cast it in a different light.

"I am indeed," she answered. "Before Yule we shall have to stop spoiling these kittens, and spoil my little one instead."

Jane nodded seriously, then fixed her with a questioning gaze. "Where's the daddy then?"

Now Marianne was disconcerted. Look where

her incautious talk had led her. "My baby's papa is gone to heaven," she said briefly. "Now, let us— "

"Then it will be wicked like us and must be sold," Charlie said matter-of-factly, as he munched a tart.

Jane nodded. "Aye, 'tis so," she sighed.

"Whatever do you mean?" Marianne gasped.

"It's what Auld Peg said. Babies without daddies are wicked and must be sold, like me and Becky. That's how we come to Auld Peg."

"Me and Charlie, too," George informed her. "It could be a sweep or maybe a rag-picker."

A shudder coursed through Marianne. That little children should be told they were wicked! That they should be told such lies! She took a breath before she spoke. "Then you must know it is false, Jane, for you have said Old Peg was a liar. Oh, it is all lies. Charlie, George, forget what you have heard. All babies are good and sweet— let us say no more about it."

Jane pursed her lips. "What about them two?" she asked, indicating the boys with a jerk of her head. "D'you suppose they was born good and turned wicked later?"

"Of course they were! It is all mistakes that are made, not sins committed. And I do not believe they are quite wicked now," she went on, "merely bored."

"Aye, that's it," Charlie nodded, "though we get some fun from watchin' old Haggerty over t' the reverend's. He says things as makes us laugh."

George chuckled. "Only today he swore he would toss us on the coals and make us into shoes for the old white horse."

Marianne could only imagine what sort of tricks they must have been up to prompt such a threat. "Perhaps," she said tentatively, "you should come here to learn your letters, like Jane and Becky."

The boys wrinkled their noses, but before they could object to this plan, Jane pronounced, *"That* wouldna do at all!"

Charlie and George glanced to the doorway just then, and Marianne followed their gaze. There stood the doctor, his arms folded and a grim expression cast over his features. How much had he heard, she wondered? None of it was to the good, she knew. He had asked her to teach the little girls their letters, not fill their heads with ideas society would never accept. Their words merely reflected what all the world thought, and she had called the world a pack of liars— and so they were. Her chin lifted a fraction. He could take issue with her if he so desired, but she would not take back a word.

"Good afternoon," he said, nodding to her. "Come, children, you have imposed on Mrs. Glencoe long enough. Say your thank yous and come along."

Jane and Becky stood and straightened their frocks before each dropped in a little curtsey. The boys likewise struggled to their feet and executed enthusiastic, if angular, bows.

"Thank you for the fine story," George said.

"And the tarts," his brother added.

"Missus Glencoe says she will tell us more stories, Dr. Venables," Jane told him. "That is kind in her, d'you not think?"

"Very kind indeed," he concurred briefly. "Now come along. Mrs. Maiden has tasks for you all."

Marianne watched the children troop out with a mixture of relief and chagrin. She did not know quite how to characterize what had just passed, nor what to expect from the doctor. Perhaps he would not let them come again. Her heart sank. She would miss them.

"You did not tell me you were a miracle worker," the doctor said quietly when they were left alone.

She stole a glance at him and was relieved to see the ghost of a smile tracing his lips. "I do not believe I have seen Charlie and George so still," he said, "and they were not asleep. And was that little Becky's voice I heard as I came in?"

So he had been there that long. She nodded, unsure how to respond. The silence that interposed was past bearing. "I am sorry, doctor. I did not mean to say such things. That is, I did, but— "

"Mrs. Glencoe, Mrs. Glencoe," he whispered. Then he took her hand in his and, raising it to his lips, kissed it as if it were the dearest thing on earth.

Eleven

It had, in fact, been Mr. Haggerty's much aggrieved tale of George's and Charlie's mischief which had sent Dr. Venables in search of the boys. Their antics had resulted in a day's work undone for the poor fellow, and his resulting wrath was understandable. Venables had followed their trail (marked by various and sundry complaints likewise vexing) from the Wallers' all the way to Rosewood Cottage. When he had reached his destination, however, the sound of Mrs. Glencoe's voice as she told her tale had transfixed him. The fairy tale, while diverting enough on its surface, spoke volumes of experience and pain, and was overlain by a mantle of wisdom.

And when she had answered the children's oddly sorted questions, the passion in her voice had etched itself on his heart. He knew that, in listening to what had passed, he had been granted the privilege of viewing a window to her soul. But it was a dark window, and only a few vague shapes were visible there.

Only one who had been accused of wickedness, accused unjustly, would rise thus to the defense of the innocent. Others might voice such sentiments. Those who felt them were rare. He knew this from the world. He knew it from himself.

Before him on the path, the children walked in pairs, Jane and Becky hand in hand, huddled together against the wind. George and Charlie, however, clasped theirs behind them, whistling tunes up into the trees, affecting innocence. For all the trials they might occasion, he agreed with the lady. He knew there was no true wickedness in any child. When her listeners had prattled on about the selling of children, a wound had opened in his heart. Mrs. Glencoe's words were balm.

What was it he felt for her? he wondered. He realized he knew little of her, little he could articulate. But what was it Pascal had said? *La coeur a ses raisons que la raison ne connaît point.* The heart has reasons of which reason knows nothing. In the past he had known a great deal about many women: their families, their fortunes, their likes and dislikes. He had known them to a nicety. Everything and nothing.

Of Mrs. Glencoe he knew nothing— and everything. Everything that mattered. She was kind and intelligent and wise. She had suffered, and went on bravely. She was beautiful, but unselfconscious. Their short acquaintance had opened for his perusal a full biography of her soul.

Unless he exercised great care, he knew he would find himself in love with her. Perhaps he already was. But that was beside the point. It would be the height of selfishness to intrude on her. Like him, she had found a refuge from the world in these hills, and it was ill conceived to think he had any right to insinuate himself on her privacy.

But there was a distinct pang as he thought of keeping his distance from her. Now that he had admitted to himself what his feelings might be, the notion nagged like a sore tooth he could not leave alone.

The children, he noticed, were now walking much closer together. That was unusual as, for the most part, the girls had kept their distance from Charlie and George. They seemed to exchange a word or two, then more. Not more mischief, he hoped. He had counted on Jane and Becky to be quiet additions to his household, peaceful foils to their noisome counterparts. He had even hoped they might confer some of their own docility on his other charges. He prayed that the opposite might not be true.

He quickened his step to catch up, but found they fell to silence at his approach. He did note, however, that Becky glanced to Jane, who in turn hissed at the boys and put a finger to her lips. What such complicity might betoken, he dared not guess.

"How are your studies progressing?" he asked Jane.

"I know my letters," she said with pride, "and Missus says I shall soon have words and stories."

"Capital! That is very good indeed."

"I should like to have stories in my head for

the dark nights," she said wistfully. "I could whisper them to Becky when we are lonely."

Poor little mite! he thought with a pang. "That would be well, but you must know, most people read stories from books."

She frowned. "They are very hard to carry about, though. Besides, if they were in my head, no one could steal them from me."

He felt his heart lurch at these words. "You needn't worry about that anymore, Jane. You know no one will steal from you here."

"Aye, I know that well enough, but who knows what tomorrow might bring?" she asked philosophically. "*You* might chuck us out, same as another. Books would be a might burden on the road, and in such weather as this."

He took her by the shoulders and knelt by her side, despite the damp of the road. "Believe me, Jane. I do not find treasures merely to cast them aside."

She managed a smile for him, an expression which did not seem to reflect her being wholly convinced. He was about to reassure her, but now Charlie tugged at his sleeve. Dr. Venables looked into a pair of worried brown eyes.

"Please, doctor," he asked, "what d'you do with them that's not treasures?"

Dr. Venables had been planning to deliver a lecture to the boys in private, but now he wondered what effect it might have. Convince them of their wickedness? That he could not do. He deliberated a moment longer.

"Tell me, boys. Have you ever heard the phrase 'a diamond in the rough'?" he asked.

Charlie looked to George. They shook their heads.

"It means that sometimes," he said slowly, "appearances are deceiving. Do you see this ring?"

He held out his hand before the children. On it, a diamond set in gold sparkled in the waning light. "This belonged to my great-grandfather. It sat many years in a vault, growing dull and tarnished. When I first saw it, I thought it a worthless trifle, but when it was polished, it proved to be quite valuable. Beneath the grime and years was a diamond waiting to sparkle. You two are the same."

The boys looked at him in disbelief, and Jane was unkind enough to make a scornful little noise. "I saw a glimpse of your sparkle today," he went on, "in Mrs. Glencoe's drawing room. You were well behaved and polite, as I have never before seen you. After what I had just heard from Mr. Haggerty, I was unprepared for such a display."

The boys hung their heads, and the doctor allowed the silence to hang in the air a moment. "Mayhap," Charlie ventured at last, "Missus brings out the shine in us?"

"Mayhap," the doctor nodded, "in all of us." Glancing up at the sky, he went on, "Let us hurry along then, before it rains again."

* * *

As soon as the doctor and the children were out of sight, Marianne took a shawl and dashed out the door in the opposite direction. Despite the wild weather, she needed a ramble in the late autumn fields to clear her head and soothe her heart. The path she followed led away from the stone circle, and that was just as well, for it now held a memory which would likely obscure her thoughts.

The hills rolled before her one after another, dotted with brush and gorse, and she wound her way between them, following the path of a small stream. The air and landscape were fresh from the storm, but they did little to calm her. The echoes of her own voice speaking to the children twined themselves into an unsteady, shifting memory of what had passed.

The words she had spoken were so flagrantly unconventional, so incautious, she trembled to recall them. How much of herself must she have revealed? No facts, of course— but her spirit had been laid bare all the same. One as perceptive as Dr. Venables must surely read something of her secrets there. Further contact with him had revealed him as far more than the lighthearted flirt she had first encountered. He was a man of knowledge and depth, one who was both learned and, in a way, naive. Still, he had not reacted in the way she feared.

Her hand still burned from his kiss. Breathless, she sank down on a low stone wall and pressed her hand against a cool cheek. His gesture was not mere gallantry— her heart told her that much—but what could he have meant by it? She did not like to think. Men had been easily smitten by her in the past, and here was a man alone, with few for company and conversation. If, incomprehensibly, he did share certain sympathies with her, it could be he was in danger of fancying himself in love with her. That would never, never do. She had made no plans for such a contingency, had never allowed for the possibility. Oh, what was she to do?

"Good morrow, mistress."

She looked up, surprised to see that Maggie had joined her, silent as a cat. She had not encountered the herb woman since their first meeting, though she had intended to find her direction.

"You've not been drinking the tea I prescribed—I can see it in your eyes. And what has brought such a fevered look to you?"

Marianne thought she discerned a twinkle in the old woman's eyes, almost as if she suspected what had sent her out into the inclement weather.

"As ever," she returned with a brief smile, "it is life."

Maggie nodded her head sagely. "Life spins a tangled skein, I know well enough. Come sit by my fire and have a sup of tea with me. The wind is almost spent, and I think there will be but one more shower this day."

Maggie led her around a bend in the stream to a grove where a small thatched cottage stood, like a picture from a book of fairy tales. Inside, a low heath fire burned, and from the rafters hung row after row of fragrant herbs, dried and bundled together. The old woman bade her sit down before the hearth, while she set the kettle to boil.

Marianne glanced about the cottage. All was neat and orderly. A bright curtain was drawn back by a ribbon to reveal an alcove with a bed. A few pieces of clothing hung from pegs on the wall. Against one wall stood a table, by far the largest piece of furniture in the dwelling. On it lay a pile of fresh cuttings, a roll of twine, a mortar and pestle, and several jars and bottles. Most interesting, however, was a shelf overflowing with books. The light was too dim to peruse their titles, but they looked old and well used.

"You shall see them another time," Maggie said, following her gaze. Marianne blushed, suddenly conscious that she had been staring quite rudely.

"Forgive me," she said. "I did not mean to— "

Maggie shook her head. " 'Tis nothing. I'd do the same myself." She took a seat across from her guest and crumbled some herbs into the teapot. "This path has led many a troubled soul to Maggie's door," she remarked quietly as she prepared the tea. "Do you wish to speak, or leave your troubles to the silence?"

Marianne sat mutely. Though she would have liked to unburden herself to someone, she knew it was not possible. The only sound was the hissing of the tea kettle and the sputter of fire. Maggie waited calmly, and at last poured the boiling water into the pot and set it on the hearth to brew.

Marianne swallowed hard. "It is . . . I cannot . . ." Her voice trailed off.

"Do not trouble yourself," the old woman told her. "You've enough on your shoulders. You'll bear up well enough, I can see— but I also see you suffer where you shouldn't."

Marianne looked into the old woman's eyes. Maggie could not possibly know or understand her burdens, yet her eyes conveyed a sympathy which belied that fact.

"You have not asked me for advice," Maggie said as she poured the tea, "but I shall give you some just the same. It is as the poet said, 'Let the dead past bury its dead, and fear ye not to speak the truth.' Now drink up your tea and think on what I have said."

Marianne sat transfixed. "How is it," she asked hollowly, "you know to say this to me?"

The old woman shrugged and looked into the flames. "It is no secret. I listen to what my heart tells me, to what your heart tells me."

"That is no answer," Marianne whispered.

The old woman looked up and caught her eye. "Trust me. It is like the weather outside. There will be a few more stormy gusts before the sun shines through, but shine it will, mistress. A little while longer, then you may dare to be happy."

Marianne felt the tears prick at her eyes. She brushed them away quickly with the back of her hand.

"You know, to cry is not a bad thing always," the woman told her. "It is sometimes a better medicine than any man has yet devised."

Marianne shook her head. "But I am not sad . . . not precisely sad. Wrought up, I suppose, and longing for the end of strife. I thought if I came so far I might have peace, but now it is broken up."

"If it's strife you're meant to have, why it will find you in London or the wilds of the west country. You cannot outrun it. Only change its guise sometimes." She laid a warm hand on Marianne's icy one. "But I suspect there's more to what's troubling you than merely strife. You are stronger than that, my dear. It is your life about to change again. There are some of us whom souls are sent to— souls whom we teach, and those we learn from."

"Of course," Marianne said, sipping at the fragrant tea and thinking of the children who had lately occupied her attention. And her baby would soon be there. That would be change.

"Aye," Maggie nodded. "It is a change for a babe to go from womb to breast, but I see more than that on your road ahead."

Life's road had already been fraught with so many twists and unexpected detours. Marianne sighed. "No peace in sight?" she asked.

Beside her, Maggie patted her hand once more. "Not all change is bad, you know. And I do not need to read your tea leaves to see your future. There is one drawn to you like moth to flame. He cannot fight it, though I sense he tries. You are a key for him, and he for you. If you would be wise," she said, "look into your heart and see what's true."

Twelve

In the days that passed, the weather grew cooler still. The wind carried on it the scent of dry leaves, although most had already fallen and become part of the fading landscape. To Marianne, it seemed that the sky itself was more meek than it had been the days before. All through the garden, the vestiges of flowers grew more brown and ragged, offering nothing but the hope of spring. The garden was a part of her now, a reflection, and her work there had helped her make the transition from the old life to the new. Within its confines, she had transformed herself from a gilded butterfly to a country matron.

As she strolled among the tattered flower beds, she looked down at her hands. It was satisfying to see they had in a very short time acquired some roughness. They were no longer remnants of a life of ease, white and useless. They had spaded dirt, weeded, planted bulbs. Come April, she reflected, living things would spring to life because of her work. She felt an intense sense of accomplishment at the notion.

Though the year was ending, the promise of

new life sustained her. As her babe grew within her, as each movement brought fresh evidence of its progress, she felt a corresponding sense of new life. The old was a cast-off shell, a husk that might be scattered and blown away by the new wind that breezed through her life. She was no longer troubled by snatches of the past in her dreams. She had packed away her mementos in the attic, and determined not to look into those trunks again.

Even though each day took her closer and closer to her baby's birth, she could not help but face the change in weather with spirits slightly flagging. Dark winter days filled only with reading and needlework would pass far more slowly than those filled with bright sunlight and fresh air. Given the almost daily visits by the four children, however, there was little chance of boredom. She recognized now what a godsend the children and their lessons represented.

They had not come today, for Becky and Jane had the sniffles and Mrs. Maiden, noting the uncharacteristic quiet of the boys, diagnosed them as sickening as well. Marianne knew well enough that her present condition demanded she keep her distance from them, but she missed the children more than she had thought possible. Though they drained her reserves of energy with their liveliness and questions, they brought with them a camaraderie, too, a sense of belonging she had missed through most of her life. Sometimes the doctor came with them when they called to take their lessons, other times he sent them on their own. When he did come, he listened to their recitations with grave attention, and often brought books for her own enjoyment.

These were not, she was happy to note, of such an improving nature as might prove to be a burden to her. They were, for the most part, accounts of travel to strange lands, but there were novels and some poetry as well. They took her away, not only from her current surroundings, but from her past as well, and she was glad of them.

There was, however, no repetition of the preference she thought he had sometimes evidenced for her. His eyes seemed always to be upon her, but that was all. He said very little and rarely stayed long. Whether it was the presence of the children or something else, she could not believe it was merely her imagination that he had become more guarded in her presence.

Maggie must have been wrong in her predictions and assessments, she concluded. It had been so easy, sitting in the woman's rustic cottage drinking tea, to believe every word that was spoken. It was not like Marianne to be so incautious as to believe the solitary fate of her heart might change. She was glad to know she had kept her own counsel.

Marianne was relieved, too, at the doctor's change in manner. For the most part. The wise part. Something deep inside, however, was overcast by the shadow of disappointment. She was both chagrined and surprised to discover that the whisper of a tendre had found its way into the withered region of her heart. Dr. Venables's image had begun to find its way there all too often. It was a good thing, she knew, that she had discovered her inclination and uprooted it like a deceptively pretty little weed which might, unchecked, work its tendrils into her well-guarded sensibilities.

She knew she could never again, in good faith, encourage any man's attention; neither could she, for her child's sake, reveal her past, regardless of how understanding such a man might appear to be. She had received the cut direct often enough to know that there was no forgiveness in the eyes of society. She must be content with the life she had created for herself, with her independence, for that much she was convinced she had achieved.

Still, when she did not guard against the occasion, her thoughts returned again and again to the doctor. It seemed ironic that, as she and Venables came to know one another better, their encounters should grow increasingly formal. She would not have guessed that the smiling gentleman who had charmed her in the stone circle could grow so distant. Perhaps it was her increasing size, she thought wryly. Each morning her glass reminded her that she could not consider herself to be the object of flirtation; she looked, she was certain, like an ungainly ship under full sail. Any attention which came her way must surely be interpreted as that displayed for ailing grandams.

Marianne wandered idly to the corner of the garden where an old apple tree leaned against the wall. The withered vestiges of its fruit hung from the upper branches and a pair of noisy blackbirds were making a feast there. All of nature seemed to have its place here. She had been unaware of it in London, where growing things were trained to the will of gardeners, and even the birds seemed as unremarkable and quiet as staid footmen.

"Meow!"

Marianne peered up into the gnarled branches. Just above her head, little Falstaff clung desperately, his eyes squeezed shut and his claws tenaciously gripping the bark. Half-grown now, his awkward legs trembled from this untoward exertion. The most adventurous of the three kittens, he often hazarded the varied entertainments the little garden offered, and, just as often, went missing for hours at a time.

"Now what mischief have you found, my little one?" she crooned, gazing up at him.

"Meow!" came his plaintive response.

She sighed and shook her head. "This is a sad predicament indeed! Let us see if I can contrive to rescue you."

She stood on tiptoe and reached upward, straining to touch the kitten. Just as she was within reach, he scuttled upward further, mewing piteously and twitching his tail. She stepped up on a twisted root and struggled to gain an inch or two. It made her a trifle dizzy to stand thus, reaching up for so long, but the imp was so close! Not close enough, however. She lowered her arms and leaned her head for a moment against the trunk of the tree. As she rested there, and allowed her body to relax, she was suddenly seized with a violent cramp in her back.

The pain seared through her, and the suddenness of it sent a tremor of fear up her spine. The kitten was forgot. What could be wrong? Her dizziness growing, she sank to her knees. Now the heady smell of apples where they had fallen to the ground and begun to rot sent an intense wave of nausea through her. She pulled a lavender-scented handkerchief from her sleeve and breathed through it, succeeding only to make matters worse.

"Mrs. Glencoe! What is amiss?"

Vaguely, she heard the gate flung open, then footsteps hurrying toward her across the lawn. In a moment, she felt an arm about her shoulders and a hand at her wrist.

"Be still and take slow deep breaths."

Venables knelt at her side, his eyes dark with concern. He said nothing more for the moment, but merely held her. She leaned back against his shoulder, drawing strength from his solidity. Her heart, which had been beating rapidly, began to slow, but she still felt far from well.

Struggling to rise, she groaned, "I must get away from these apples. The smell of them is making me ill."

"When you feel equal to it," he said, "let me know, and I shall carry you indoors."

She shook her head weakly. "That will not be necessary," she protested. "Please, just allow me another moment to collect myself."

Glancing about, he saw that the French doors to the drawing room were closest and slightly ajar. "Please, madam," he said softly, "you must permit me what gallantry occasion offers a doctor."

Lifting her in his arms against her slight protests, he made in the direction of the house. She seemed little heavier than a kitten, and the way she curled into his arms and rested her head against his shoulder reminded him of a sleepy child being carried off to the nursery. Still, he was not altogether unaware of the softness of her form, or the scent of verbena which drifted up to him. He steeled himself against such wayward thoughts and made his way as quickly as he might toward the house. When he reached the doors, he pushed one of them open with his boot and set her gently down on a sofa.

He watched anxiously as she leaned gingerly back into the cushions and shut her eyes. "Tell me what happened," he said after a moment. "You looked quite gray a moment ago, but your color is returning."

Briefly, she described what had taken place in the garden, her voice edged with anxiety. "I do not mean to make much of such a small thing, and it is passing now, but it was such a very violent pain. Tell me, doctor," she asked, as she concluded her narrative. "Ought I to be alarmed?"

He shook his head and smiled at her, hoping

to dispel the fear he saw reflected in her large eyes. "I suspect it is merely one of the many difficulties that men are spared. It is quite common for expectant mothers to suffer such painful spasms. Your back is not accustomed to carrying the extra weight."

"Ah," she sighed. "I had begun to wonder if there were not some price to be paid for the little miracle housed within me! And there is worse to come, unless I have heard amiss."

"Unfortunately, that is quite true," he told her. "But do not forget, I have seen many babes born. They are indeed miracles, full of the future. Yours will be no different. Nature has thus contrived to make the memory of the pain of labor fade quickly— once the mother has laid eyes on her precious packet."

"And very wise is nature," she returned with some asperity, "else women would never be persuaded to bear more than one!"

"Very likely not," he agreed judiciously. "Shall I order some tea for you, while I rescue little Falstaff? It was he, was it not?"

"Heavens!" she cried. "I had forgot all about the scamp. Oh, please do!"

He opened the connecting door and made his request to Annie, who happened just then to be passing by. Then he proceeded through the French doors into the garden once again, leaving her deep in thought.

Though Marianne had not before today discussed her condition with the doctor— nor indeed had he pressed her to do so— his manner and smile when he did so just now seemed to reflect far more than just professional interest. His anxiety was as real as hers, and when he had, for a moment, let down his guard, he seemed unaccountably to share in her joy. What sort of man, she wondered, rejoiced in the mere notion of new life, in the quickening of a child not his own? She could not begin to understand him, but it was little wonder that one such as he pursued his life and dreams beyond the brittle cynicism of the *ton,* where children were merely security for ancient titles and the building of fortunes.

The doctor returned a moment later, bearing the prodigal on his shoulder. He set the kitten back in the basket with his siblings, where he curled into a ball and went to sleep, apparently unrepentant.

"I do not wish to unnecessarily concern you, Mrs. Glencoe," he said when he had seated himself, "and I recognize you are not my patient. But it is important for you to begin paying more attention to your symptoms and act on them accordingly. Ladies who have led quiet lives, as you seem to have done, tend to be more delicate, more prone to discomforts, than those who are used to exertion. I believe that Old Maggie will attend you very well when your time comes, but in the interim you must be careful. Do not overtire yourself. Do not go farther than your voice might be heard, should you be overcome again. And," he added with a twinkle, "you must be sure to ask for assistance the next time you are called upon to rescue a kitten."

"Yes," she said. "Of course, you are right. I have undergone some similar dizziness in the past, and a little nausea, but not quite so violent as today. I rather think the pain must have made everything else seem worse. I must thank you for your concern."

"Nonsense," he said brusquely. "It is my work." He patted her hand. Against his own, it seemed tiny, like that of a doll. "Besides, it is I who must thank you. During these dreary days of applying poultices and setting bones, it is not often the occasion arises that I may exercise my dusty sense of chivalry."

"Nor," she replied with a slight smile, "have I been much accustomed to being rescued in quite such a dashing manner!"

"Ah, so all your rescues have been commonplace?"

"They tend to be," she said archly, "when one is forced to perform them herself."

He would like to have pursued this interesting comment when the door opened and Annie entered, balancing a tray carefully. It was laden not only with a pot and cups, but a plate of scones, marmalade, and cream, as well. "Cook thought you might be in need of sustenance, ma'am. She declares you are too thin."

"Take it away, Annie," her mistress said, turning from the sight. "I could not possibly . . .

The doctor looked at her narrowly. "Perhaps later then. Just set the tray on the table, Annie.

Your cook is a wise woman, Mrs. Glencoe," he told her. "In my experience, thin mamas bear thin babies, and we cannot have that. Annie, I have left my bag in the garden. Will you fetch it for me?"

When Annie had set about this errand, he once more directed a critical eye at Marianne. "Have you been eating regularly and well?"

"As well as I am able," she responded. "Sometimes, I must confess, I feel as if I will eat everything in the pantry—the curry you were so kind to bring did not see the end of that day, I can assure you—but there are other times I am not equal to a single bite."

He pressed his lips together into a frown. Women, he knew, suffered from a variety of odd humors during these last months. Chances were that all was well. Still, it was best in these matters to be prudent. "I hope you will not think me impertinent, but I think it would be wise if I conducted an examination—just to be certain all is progressing normally. These late months of a pregnancy can sometimes be difficult."

Marianne leaned back into the sofa and shut her eyes for a moment. It was foolish to think she could go much longer without the doctor's suggesting such an examination, and certainly not after the state in which he had discovered her today. If anything were amiss, she must learn what it was. Still, the notion of submitting to such a procedure rattled her at her core. She was haunted by that fear, foolish or not, that signs of her past could be read on her body. What if he could tell, could see?

Annie set the doctor's bag inside the door just then, and stood waiting. Marianne shook herself and nodded.

"There is no hurry, Mrs. Glencoe," the doctor told her. "Do you think you could manage a cup of tea?"

"I am ready now," she said resolutely.

"I shall not be very long about this I promise, Mrs. Glencoe," he said briskly, taking up his bag. "Shall we adjourn to your chamber?"

His innocent suggestion reverberated with painful memories, and she revisited with painful clarity all those moments in the past when drawing room conversation had been a mere prelude. Would there never be an end to this sensation of the past reliving itself in new contexts? It was all so awkward, so unnerving, and the doctor's vitality, his courtliness, his physical presence only underscored these sensations. If only the doctor were some prosing Methuselah, she might not be reminded of these persistent ghosts!

Marianne pressed her lips together and arose without comment, preceding him from the room. Just as she gathered up the hem of her heavy black skirts to ascend the staircase, the doctor asked, "Will you have Annie attend you, or have you a personal maid?"

Surely he knew she did not. Marianne gripped the banister as she felt the blood rush to her cheeks. So much for her pains! How could she have forgot such a simple thing as not allowing a gentleman, even a doctor, to accompany her to her chamber without another woman in attendance? Her heart pounded as the impropriety into which she had almost allowed herself to fall struck her.

She did not turn, however, merely paused a brief moment before replying, "Annie, of course, will come." Then she continued to make her way up the stairs.

A little while later, Marianne shivered behind a screen while Annie helped her remove her gown and wrapped a shawl about her, over her chemise. The doctor, she could see, stood gazing out the window, waiting for her to be ready. She stepped into the room resolutely and sat herself down on the edge of the bed. All I must do, she thought, is think on good things. Ignore everything else. Think about next summer's flowers, the birds. Think about my baby.

She lay down on the bed and turned her eyes to the wall.

Thirteen

As Dr. Venables drove home, his thoughts were oddly sorted. In past weeks, the doctor had watched as Mrs. Glencoe hugged herself at the mention of her babe, radiant with the sensation of life within her, and had felt a familiar tug at his heart. Watching the ghost of sorrow fade from her countenance was part of what sent his footsteps in her direction day after day. He had been careful not to reveal his emotions, however. The stricken look in her eyes the day he had so rashly kissed her hand had haunted him ever since. What secrets lay behind those fathomless blue eyes? he wondered.

What had really sent her from the embrace of the *ton* to the wilds of Cornwall? For him, this had been a place of healing. Years ago, the open fields and the sound of the sea had acted as a balm on his shattered soul. Time after time, he had observed the serenity of the place soothe others. Here, he had seen the beasts and children heal their wounds as well.

It was the same with Mrs. Glencoe. With Marianne. As he observed her, first with the kittens, then in tutoring the children, he hardly noticed her beauty anymore. It was rather like the feeling one had in summer; after the joy of spring, summer's beauty was both accepted and expected for the gift it was, but rarely remarked upon. Whenever he could find an excuse to do so, Venables had basked in the glow of Marianne's goodness, her intelligence, and growing humor.

He ought not, he knew, to trail after one so newly widowed, and he hoped that his motive in finding his way so often to her door was not as transparent as he feared. Though he had, as yet, turned from the question of whether or not he were in love with her, he knew he was fascinated by the lady, at ease in her company, and nervous as a cat when he was not. If only the same were true of her. She had, he thought, begun to warm toward him, but he had spoiled it all by acting unwisely, grasping for a happiness which might never be allowed him. All too often of late she had seemed abstracted and overwrought in his presence; never more so than today.

A physical examination was never comfortable for ladies, but there was something exceedingly odd about the one he had just conducted. Odd from the start. Odd that Marianne should have forgot to request the maid to accompany her. No lady, widow or otherwise, would have dreamed of placing herself in such a position. Though he had little patience with such conventions, and would certainly not have condemned her for her oversight, he knew such habits died hard.

But still, he argued with himself, she is pregnant and newly widowed. Either such eventuality would be sufficient to make a lady forgetful. He shook his head. Ladies might forget where they had left their embroidery silk or workbasket, but the deportment lessons of their governesses and mamas, never. Though her voice and manner clearly revealed she had sprung from the highest circles, something, he felt in his heart, had happened to her. Something more than the death of a husband (particularly one who seemed to be mourned not at all) had interrupted the custom of one sort of life and replaced it with another. She seemed to live between worlds, this Mrs. Glencoe from nowhere in particular.

What nagged at him the most as he drove through the deepening twilight was her manner during the examination itself. How could that be accounted for? he wondered. He had expected the reluctance, the embarrassment other ladies had in the past exhibited. But there were no blushes, no demurring. She had simply lain herself upon the bed quite passively, and turned her head away from him. She had shown not the least response when he placed his hands upon her abdomen to ascertain the child's size and position, nor when he rested his head against her bosom to listen to her heart. When his examination had become even more intimate, she had not even twitched. It was as if she had taken her*self* away, as if only her body were there. In India, he had often witnessed such detachment, but never in England, never in a woman.

Then it struck him. There had been such a woman. Good God, he had almost forgot her. It was when he had first begun to study medicine. He had accompanied old Dr. Thurlow on his rounds down the filthy back lanes of London. He was desperate to help the wretches he saw there, yet too green to prevent averting his eyes from their misery at every turn.

A child had grasped Thurlow's arm and all but pulled him up a narrow flight of stairs to a hovel that passed as home for seven other children and their consumptive mother. She strained fitfully against her labor pains, but made not a sound. It was clear as soon as they saw her emaciated body that neither she nor the infant would have the strength to live. When Thurlow placed a hand on her abdomen, the woman had turned away unseeing, unfeeling, as if accepting whatever the touch might bring for good or ill.

Today, he had recognized that same dispassionate resignation in Mrs. Glencoe. There the resemblance ended, but it seemed to him that some history, some similar incident of hard usage must connect the two women in spirit. It chilled his heart to recall the similar expression on their faces, the vulnerability of their bodies. This was what men did to women. A shaft of anger pierced his heart. Perhaps, he concluded grimly, that was the reason no trace of Mrs.

Glencoe's late husband was in evidence. She did not wish to remember him.

It seemed, then, that she bore the burden of secrets, and bore it close— as he did his. He shook his head. He had no right to pry into the lives of his patients— for that was what she was. He could claim no more of her. His only duty was to heal and ease pain. That must be sufficient.

When he entered his home, he at once encountered Mrs. Maiden, who was balancing a heavily laden tray as she embarked on the stairs.

"Good evening, Mrs. Maiden," he said. "How fare our patients?"

"They are trying mine," she said darkly.

He raised his eyebrows. Though he did not wish anyone ill, he had hoped, unwisely it now seemed, that the children abed might be less trouble to his housekeeper than they were afoot. "What have they been about?"

"Eating!" she pronounced. "They do not have the appetites of sickly children, for all they cough and sneeze. This is the fifth tray I have carried up this day. Why do they not sleep, like other invalids?"

Venables laughed. "I see they are not on the verge of turning up their toes!"

"No, indeed," blowing a stray wisp of graying hair out of her eyes, "although I may do so well enough before this day is done!"

He shrugged off his coat and hung it over the

stair rail. "Here," he said, reaching for the tray. "Rest yourself. I shall carry it up this time."

As he made his way up the stairs, he could hear a low whispering coming from the chamber the girls shared. He stood outside the door for a moment, listening. Charlie and George were closeted there as well. What were they up to now? A few words drifted toward him in Jane's soft Scottish lilt, ". . . then 'tis best we dinna wait till that baby's born." Then one of the boys seemed to second her suggestion. His curiosity racing, he cleared his throat, waited for silence, and entered the little room.

All four of them, he noted, had runny noses, and greeted him with a simultaneous sniffle. Venables set the tray on a table and surveyed his charges. Their eyes flickered one to the other. Clearly they were up to something, despite their shared malady.

"Have you brought more scones?" George asked, his eyes wide and innocent. "And lots of cream? Last time there was not enough cream."

"I see you are becoming accustomed to this life of ease," Venables said, schooling a smile into a grim line.

"Let me feel your foreheads." He did so, noting they were all as cool as cucumbers. "As I suspected, you are clearly on the mend."

"Aye, 'tis so," Charlie sighed. "Mrs. Maiden has already told me more than once today that 'tis only the good dies young."

"And you are looking forward to living to a ripe old age, are you?"

"Aye, but come to think of it, Mrs. Maiden must be very wicked then, doctor, for she is so old she creaks when she walks."

Venables was forced to cough up his sleeve to hide his laughter, for the sound of Mrs. Maiden's rusty stays did indeed echo through the passages. "Ahem," he managed. "Let us have no talk of who is and who is not wicked, for you must know that age is nothing to do with it. There is no reason to be looking forward to your dotage."

"Is that what we've got instead of scones?" Charlie asked incredulously. "But I asked especially—"

"Hush," the doctor chuckled. He lifted the cloth from the tray. "Mrs. Maiden, as you can readily see, is the soul of goodness. Here are sufficient scones and cream and strawberry jam for all of you to make yourselves exceedingly sticky."

When they were busily munching away, he said quite casually, "Suppose you all tell me what you were plotting just now?"

The boys, intriguers of old, maintained surprised expressions with admirable tenacity, but Jane swallowed backward with surprise and had to be clapped upon the back quite soundly, to check her startled coughing.

"Looby," Charlie hissed under his breath.

She shook her red curls and made a face at him. "I couldna help it," she snapped back.

"Girls never can," he said disgustedly. "It was plum mad I was to ever think I could trust—"

"Aye," she interrupted, "you've said it yourself, you're a bedlamite— you and that brother of yours. Crazy as March hares, the two o' you.''

"Hey now!" Charlie objected, clearly pained to be included in this invective. "I didn't say nothin', you— you— orphan!"

Jane's eyes flashed. "Becky 'n' me'll have our own plan, and we needn't be bothered wi' the likes o' you. It's not orphans we'll be much longer, and you needna think you'll be included."

The threesome looked daggers at one another, while Venables, much intrigued, waited for their explanation. It was not forthcoming. All this while, Becky had said nothing, merely glanced from one combatant to the next, as if she were nothing more than a polite observer at a game of shuttlecock which had got out of hand. She shook her head ruefully at them. Then she glanced at the doctor and tugged at his sleeve.

"A word wi' ye, sir?" Becky whispered.

Until this moment, the child had never before addressed him beyond an occasional monosyllable. She must consider the import of what she had to convey to be earth-shattering indeed. He nodded a fraction in her direction, then addressed Charlie and George.

"Come, boys. Off to your own beds. You have commiserated with the young ladies long enough, and all of you need to rest, if you are to recover your strength."

"But the scones is here!" Charlie protested, much aggrieved.

"To the contrary," the doctor frowned at him.

"They are mainly inside of you and George. Now run along."

When he was left alone with the girls, Jane stared exasperatedly at Becky and whispered, "What d'you think you're about?"

"Good sense," the other retorted in her whispery little voice. "We are already discovered— 'tis best to lay the matter before him."

Jane rolled her eyes, but when she glanced up at the doctor who stood observing them in an extremely interested manner, she grinned wryly at him and said, "If you must know, doctor, we been busyin' ourselves at arrangin' your life for you!"

He lifted his brows at the revelation of the children's meddling, and shuddered to think what they must have in mind. If they had their way, he suspected they would beg him to close his surgery and open a confectionery in its stead. In the end, however, curiosity won out over the inclination to adjure them to mind their own affairs, and at last he managed a fairly steady, "Pray tell?"

" 'Tis like this," Jane began. " 'Twas easy enough to decide you must marry Mrs. Glencoe, for 'tis clear you're of a mind with us on that, but it was the when and how gave us all fits."

"Indeed? And how is it you come to know my mind to such a surety?"

Jane snorted derisively. " 'Tis easy enough to see, if a body walks about with her eyes open. When you drive by her cottage, you slow down and stare like there was a street fair to be found behind the wall.''

Venables felt the heat rise under his collar. Did he do so, truly?

"What's more," she went on, "when you sit with us there, you keep watch on her like a puir dog under the table— and see nothin' else. Why, three times Charlie has pinched George under your very eyes, and you've not seen."

Could this be true? Very likely, for he was quite fascinated by Mrs. Glencoe. But to think he had imagined he guarded his conduct with some care. The lady's preoccupied manner and sometimes faraway look had allowed him to let down his guard. Jane's eyes were sparkling mischievously at him. He sighed inwardly. Perhaps no amount of circumspection could hide what he felt from eyes determined to see.

" 'Tis the same with her as well." Jane allowed her words to hang in the air a moment. Then the child yawned and stretched. "I think I'll be havin' a bit of a nap now," she said.

Little wretch! He knew she was trying to lead him on— and was succeeding.

"Finish what you've begun," he said, stifling a groan.

Casting him a sidelong glance, she said, "Surely t' heaven you've noticed it yourself!" Beside her, Becky giggled. "But no," she continued, shaking her head. "How could you? For 'tis *after* you've left she stares out the window after you, and does not hear our questions for all we repeat them time and again."

"And so," Becky whispered, looking up at him with her huge eyes, " 'tis clear you must marry her."

"Aye," Jane nodded emphatically, "and before she has that baby."

Fourteen

It had taken no small amount of circuitous questioning before Dr. Venables could decipher the reasoning behind the girls' enigmatic pronouncement on his affairs. He had turned the matter over in his head all that night and into the morning, as he embarked on his daily journey through the countryside. He was considering it still when he found his way later in the afternoon to the residence of the Reverend and Mrs. Waller.

He entered with some diffidence, for he had of late spent so much of his time at Rosewood Cottage as to have become a near stranger at the parsonage. Still, the Wallers greeted him warmly, drew a chair for him by the fire, and made him very much at home.

"It is good to see you, doctor," Mrs. Waller told him when he was seated. "Enos and I have missed your company sorely."

"Indeed," the reverend agreed with a self-deprecating smile. "Suzannah does not care to discuss theology with me, you see, and the servants become quite distressed when I talk to myself."

Venables laughed. He had missed the Wallers'
companionship more than he had imagined.

"You think he is jesting, doctor," Mrs. Waller
interjected, "but many's the time I have threatened to purchase a talking parrot for my husband, that he might have some discourse."

"Come, my love," her husband returned, "you
know I do not like to hear my own words repeated to me. I must be argued with! Now, doctor, I must show you an edition of the works of
Duns Scotus I have been poring over. He makes
an interesting argument that— "

"Please, Enos!" Mrs. Waller interrupted, casting a long-suffering look in Venables' direction.
"Not until we have given the good doctor some
tea!"

"I am sure the doctor will be most interested,
Suzannah. Just a moment, Venables," he said,
rising, "and I shall fetch the particular volume
from the bookroom."

When the reverend had gone in search of his
book, Mrs. Waller shook her head and smiled.
"I shall be surprised, indeed," she said, "if my
husband does not lose himself in its pages and
forget about us entirely."

"We shall know in a half hour or so," Venables
teased. "He seems to have mended well. I do not
think I can betray the least sign of a limp."

"He took your advice to heart," she laughed.
"The notion of staying rooted in his library to
spare his ankle appealed to him enormously. He
was so caught up in his studies, that he forgot
entirely to write his sermon one Sunday and de-

livered one *extempore:* it was quite brief, but exceedingly well received. I think he may have learned that a few words from the heart are more convincing than hundreds of lofty sentiments."

With that she turned the conversation to news of the neighborhood: a farm had changed tenancy, and the banns were to be read for a number of young couples, but the district's most significant news was that a member of the gentry was stopping at the inn.

"Such visitors are so rare as to attract as great a crowd as a Punch and Judy show," Mrs. Waller said with a shake of her head. "I have been receiving all manner of reports on the poor gentleman's carriage and horses— even how many bottles of claret he consumed at dinner last night!"

"It is to be hoped," the doctor commented, "he is able to conduct whatever business brought him to these parts and take his leave, before he is entered as one of the sights in the guide book."

"And before Charlie and George discover a way to charge their fellows a penny apiece to have a look at him," she added with a spark of humor. "Speaking of which, how does Mrs. Glencoe fare with the children?"

"Very well indeed. It is become a perfect little world for them at Rosewood Cottage. Mrs. Glencoe, the soul of patience, allows them to run tame there. However, all of the children— Charlie and George included— are learning their letters and numbers."

Mrs. Waller very nearly choked on her tea. "Do not tell me those rapscallions have embarked on the road to scholarship! What is our dear Mrs. Glencoe's secret?"

The image of Marianne rose up before him. What could she command that any male would not be happy to perform? "I believe," he said, after a moment, "it is a combination of their having fallen a little in love with her— and knowing they have outworn their welcome at any other house in the area!"

She cast her eyes heavenward and nodded. "That is so, I am afraid. After their last visit here, our Haggerty threatened to give in his notice if they were not at once drawn and quartered!" Then her eyes twinkled at him. "It is a good thing my husband was able to convince the poor soul to moderate his view. I cannot think the magistrate would have supported Haggerty in the matter."

Venables smiled ruefully. "I collect they have never yet paid a call on our magistrate, else he would have had them behind bars ere now— and very likely have concurred with Mr. Haggerty's suggestion."

"So, they are perforce become angels. And are you able to see anything beyond that guileless surface? Do you not fear they might simply be biding their time to play some trick or other?"

The doctor began to speak, then suddenly stopped himself. He knew quite well what

they—and the girls—were up to, but did not
know how or whether to convey this information.

"Come, doctor. What is it you are not telling
me?" Mrs. Waller teased. "Trust me, I have en-
ured myself to such tales as old Mithridates to
poison. I believe there is little I cannot bear!"

"It is not precisely tricks," he said slowly, "nor
is it the boys on their own, who have entered
into a conspiracy."

"And whom else have they corrupted?" she
asked in surprise.

He frowned as he considered her question.
"Corruption is not quite the word. Nor am I
certain, in this case, that the plot was initially of
their making."

She took a deep breath. "I am afraid you must
begin at the beginning, for I am all at sea!"

"It is George and Charlie and Jane and Becky
all together, you see, setting the world straight—
at least by their childish appraisal."

She cocked her head, but looked encourag-
ingly at him as she waited for the silence to pass.
He settled back in his chair and tapped the tips
of his fingers together. "You have stood as
something of a sister to me these last years, Mrs.
Waller," he began, "else I should not know how
to tell you of this, for, believe me, this tale is
not in the least ordinary."

She smiled. "Nor did I expect it to be."

"It comes to this," he said. "I have been so
naive as to think that merely removing the children from the squalor of their surroundings,
bringing them here to the country, would be suf-

ficient to erase their past, to set them on a fresh future." He looked up and caught her astute expression. "You are correct. I was foolish to make such an assumption; as you might guess, despite my attempts at reassuring the children, they are still afraid they will be disowned, and abandoned once again to their own resourcefulness."

"Poor little waifs," she sighed. "That has, after all, been the story of their lives."

"Indeed, and it is not in the least an uncommon fate. It makes me shudder to think of them cast on the world's cold charity— and of all the others like them who suffer such treatment."

"So, tell me," she said softly, when he had been silent for a long moment, "just what is it they are about?"

"Matchmaking," he said at last with a rueful sigh. There. It was out. Let the lady make of it what she would.

"Of course," she nodded, apparently not in the least surprised. "You and Mrs. Glencoe, I presume?"

"Yes, and before her baby is born, if you can credit it! But," he stopped himself, "how did you know?"

She laughed and shook her head. "It is only what the entire district has been thinking. And the match has many fine attributes— your backgrounds are similar, you seem to rub along uncommonly well. Besides, it is a commonly held opinion that single men are in need of wives— and babies in need of fathers."

The complacency with which Mrs. Waller responded to his revelation put him to silence for a moment. Was he so unaware of his community, so oblivious to them, that their discussion of the intimate details of his life should take him by surprise? He should have known better. And as for Mrs. Waller's assessment of his situation, there was a good deal of truth to it. Certainly, he had heard of poorer reasons for marrying.

"Tell me," she said, interrupting his thoughts, "what arguments do the children offer you?"

Jane's eyes had glistened when she explained her apprehensions to him, and he felt a dull ache at the back of his throat as he recalled the scene now. "It is all fear," he said simply. "They fear that once Mrs. Glencoe's child is born, she will have neither time nor love remaining for children not her own— and they will become such a burden to me that I shall send them back to the city." He sighed. "They would have it that is why I sent them to Mrs. Glencoe to begin with."

"How silly of them," she said with an arch smile, "when all the neighborhood knows you had to do so that you might call there more frequently."

Ignoring her shrewd insight, he stood and walked to the window. The evening was gathering; it would be dark soon. "The question is," he said at last, "what am I to do? My assurances seem to mean nothing, and I cannot have the poor mites worried that they will soon be on the road."

"Forgive me for correcting you," Mrs. Waller smiled, "but the real question is: why do you not simply offer for Mrs. Glencoe?"

He turned and looked at her hard. There was no teasing in her eyes now.

"There are, of course, any number of quite practical reasons you should do so," she said, then went on softly, "but believe me, I should not suggest such a thing did I not believe you to be in love. Has not your heart yet shown you the truth of it?"

Just then, Reverend Waller reentered, bearing a dusty tome. "Forgive me, doctor," he said, as he entered. "I had quite forgot what I went to fetch. It is most annoying in me I am sure, this absentmindedness."

Venables grinned, thankful for a reprieve. "No more annoying than the color of your hair or eyes, Reverend, for it is as much a part of you."

Reverend Waller was already absorbed in finding the passage he wished to share, and did not seem to hear. But Venables could still feel Mrs. Waller's eyes on him, and knew that her unanswered question still hung in the air between them, like a thread loosened from the fabric of his own fears.

Dr. Venables turned his horse toward home as the last light disappeared to the west; he rode in uncertain spirits. Was he truly in love? Had he let down his guard so much that such a feat

as that might be accomplished? And was it so
clear that he was the only one who could not
see it? The answers came quickly: yes, yes, and
again, yes.

And what of Mrs. Glencoe? What of Marianne? The notion of waking to her smile each
day, to her bounteous kindness and beauty each
day, made his heart race. But did she, could she,
return his love? He did not know. She was like
the tide, one moment seeming to be drawn toward him, the next, drawing away. What was he
to make of her? She had her own secrets, that
much was clear— and they might remain so. He
would be untruthful to say he felt no urge to
discover what they might be, but he had no
right. Whatever the mystery might be, it had far
better rest as quiet as the late captain.

But what of his own secrets? Would she press
him for information? He thought not. But . . .
if he told, what then? Would she turn her heart
away from him, and freeze him with a stare
when she heard of his past? The thought, now
it had formed, was unbearable.

Ought he to leave well enough alone? he wondered. He did not wish to. Part of him whispered, *I can make her love me,* while another part
jeered, *make her love what?* Rationally, spiritually
even, he knew he had at last become one who
might hope for love. But that was in the daylight
hours, before his dreams haunted him.

As he rode up to the house, he could see the
curtain at the upstairs window twitch. The children were watching for him. He dismounted his

horse, wondering desperately what he might do to make it all come right.

He went straight to his study, avoiding, for the nonce, their pointed questions and penetrating stares. Solitude was little better, but at least it had no voice, no imploring look.

He leaned back in his worn leather chair and traced the line of his thin scar with his fingertips, summoning the dark and the light of his past, hoping to find some answer to his dilemma there. He remembered the inn where he had almost ended it all those many years ago . . .

Outside, a clear starry night had been at odds with the raucous noise from the public rooms below. Neither had had the least effect on him. His soul, his very body had been full of shame and regret, as his fingers had traced the form of the loaded pistol on the table. In a few moments, he would put a period to his life.

His parents would mourn, he knew, for they loved him— far too much, as it turned out. But he hoped they would see his last act as a desperate attempt to finish it all with honor, to put an end to his trail of shameless exploits, a trail which had ended in disarray, fraught with cries of pain and the uncomprehending look of a child, now crippled for life. It was those eyes which haunted his every waking hour, and the eyes of the child's parents, who dared neither speak out nor take action against the gentry.

His only hurt in the accident had been a thin

deep cut which ran from his chin to his left ear. As he fingered it in the semidarkness, Venables felt its burning sting with a sort of satisfaction. He took a long draught of water, for he would allow himself no spirits to anaesthetize his last moments. Painfully clearheaded, for once, he had picked up the pistol, raised it to his temple and . . . then, suddenly, it had been gone, disappeared into thin air, as if he were the victim of some curious parlor trick.

Astounded, he had clutched at the empty air. Then he heard a sound behind him. He whipped about, furious that he had been intruded upon. Before him, a young man sat in a chair by the fire, smiling sadly at him. The pistol was cradled in his lap.

"Pray be seated, Alden," the youth had said. "We shall talk a while, you and I."

Bereft of speech, Venables had stared mutely at him, then at the door. The bolt was still in place. "How, in God's name— ?" he began.

"Come, now" the other chided. "The *how* is the least important of your concerns. You know that quite well, do you not?"

Venables sat speechless for several minutes, contemplating the gentleman across from him. "I do not understand any of this," he whispered at last. "I do not know who you are, how you got in here, or what you mean by it, but I wish you will go away and leave me to my business."

"Of that, I have no intention . . . at least for the moment." Again, he smiled disarmingly. "Please, Alden, do me the honor of listening to me.

Then, when I have done, I promise I shall leave you to your own devices."

Bewildered, Venables sank into a chair and stared at his visitor. His hair shone gold, and his eyes were as blue as a jay's wing. His face was familiar somehow, but Alden could not put a name to him. "Who are you?" he asked hoarsely.

"You may call me Michael," came the answer. "I suggest you take a moment to recover yourself, but then you may wish to don a coat. We shall be going out."

Fifteen

Venables did not know if he believed in angels, but as he looked back on the incident, that was how he always thought of the mysterious youth. Together, they had walked through squalid streets, scenes of unbelievable deprivation: he had seen eyes empty of hope, children with twisted limbs crying themselves to sleep with hunger, wantons near-dead with fatigue, struggling to attract the attention of bored degenerates that somehow those same children might be fed and cared for.

At last, when he could stand no more, Venables had flung himself against a stone wall, covering his face. "Why do you torment me thus?" he had cried. "Am I not yet sunk deep enough that I must still endure more? Take me back, and let me put an end to at least one soul's desperate misery."

"I could allow it," the youth said with slow deliberation. "But it would be a sinful waste of your gifts, Alden. Do you not think they have been left idle long enough?"

"My *gifts!*" he sneered. "And what are they

but an overriding penchant for dissolution? Condemn me if you must, but do not mock me."

The stranger shook his head. "I do not, Alden. If you proceed with your plan, it is true you will end your own misery— for the moment. But, if not, there is much you might do. It is time on this tired old earth for those such as you to turn from selfishness to give comfort, where before you have only taken. To extend a hand and heal, where you might otherwise have hurt."

There was something in these words, in the tone in which they were spoken, that resounded in his very soul. For the first time in many weeks, his heart was lightened. He felt as if a window had been opened, and the cool fresh breeze of hope touched his heart.

"Yes," Michael had said, "there is much you might do. You cannot entirely erase the harm you have done. But you might mitigate it— and ease much of the outrage that has been caused by others."

Venables knew that the child he had injured still lived, and though he had emptied his pockets, astounding the impoverished parents with a glittering array of sovereigns, it was, he knew, an empty gesture, one which would never make amends for the harm he had done. No more would his death.

It was dawn when he found himself back at the inn. Below, the first sounds of street vendors had replaced those of the evening's revelry. Though he had not slept a wink, Venables felt refreshed and, if not full of hope, at least not wholly divorced from it. From that day he had dedicated himself to bettering the condition of those around him, had given away that part of his fortune which was not entailed, and had embarked on a study of medicine. From thence it had been a driven, but fulfilling life, haunted less and less frequently by the shadow of the past.

Michael's parting words had been, "There is no one entirely undeserving of happiness, you know. The day will arrive when happiness will take you in its embrace— and you will be able to bear it."

Staring ahead at the fire, snug in his study, Venables wondered whether that day had arrived at last.

Marianne slept late the next day, having been kept awake much of the night with a series of pains which had sent her pacing about until almost dawn. She felt better now as she enjoyed a leisurely cup of tea, but an unaccustomed lethargy persuaded her to remain abed much of the morning and even into the afternoon of a lowering stormy day.

When she did, at last, arise and find her way into the drawing room, she discovered that the doctor had called earlier and left for her a bouquet of branches hung with red berries. Annie had placed it in a vase in a prominent position, and it warmed Marianne's heart to look at it.

She had missed the color which the bouquets from her garden had provided all summer. It was like the doctor to have noticed their absence in her home of late, and to have braved the rough weather to gather these branches for her.

She had recovered her equanimity somewhat after his last visit, despite having so dreaded the inevitable examination. She had been able to remove herself from this anxiety, and now she found that only the merest whisper of that intimacy had imprinted itself on her consciousness. Her secrets were still safe. To her infinite relief, there had been nothing unusual in his tone or demeanor to suggest that he had discovered anything untoward; he had merely informed her that, in his opinion, the child would arrive sooner than she had calculated. What she recalled most about the episode was his kindness, his gentleness, and tact. He was what she had come to believe did not, could not, exist— a good man.

She closed her eyes as she felt her throat tighten. If only she might be allowed to love him, she sighed. If only she might encourage the hints she had sometimes discerned of his inclination toward her. Such thoughts, she knew, were worse than useless. Once the baby came, she hoped her heart would be full enough to forget such idle fancies. But still, she thought, she might indulge herself for the present in a harmless daydream.

She curled herself onto the sofa, tucked a rug about her, and gave her imagination full rein. She could see quite clearly how such a life might

be. How, weary after a long day's toil, Dr.
Venables, Alden, might turn to her with a smile
for comfort and ease. They would sit before a
fire, and she would take his head onto her lap,
stroke his curls, and tell him the little events of
the day. There might even be more children,
she thought wistfully.

How calm and comfortable this dream
seemed, compared to those she had conjured as
a young girl. If only she had known then what
comprised happiness. Perhaps one never knew,
not until its prospect had been rudely snatched
away.

She sighed heavily. A half-finished gown for
the baby beckoned from the sewing basket, and
she picked it up and began to stitch in a desul-
tory sort of way. It was difficult to keep her mind
on her work, however; time after time, she was
forced to reset a row of stitches. At last, she
pricked her finger painfully and threw the garment aside, anxious not to stain its snowy folds.

She glanced about the room: a book lay abandoned on the table before her, but it did not
beckon to her now, for she felt altogether too
dull to make any sense of what she read. The
fire burned brightly and did not need stoking.
A tray with her tea sat untouched before her.
Truthfully, she had no idea what would strike
her fancy.

As if in answer to her ennui, she heard the
soft rise and fall of voices in the entry. It was
Jane and Becky. Surely it was not wise, she
thought as she regarded the gray sky beyond the

window, to allow them about on so stormy a day. When Annie ushered them in, their cheeks and noses rosy with the cold, she exclaimed, "Great heavens! Go at once and stand before the fire and warm yourselves."

She shooed them forward, relieved them of their wraps, and handed them to the maid. "Indeed," she said, "I do not know what Mrs. Maiden is about, letting you out into the cold."

"Pooh!" Jane cried. " 'Tis nothing! For you see we have warm clothes and even boots." She displayed these for Marianne with evident pride. "Besides," she went on, " 'twas not Mrs. Maiden, but the doctor himself who sent us here to see how you got on. It was very kind in him, d'you not think?"

"Indeed it was," Marianne said. "But I think it wisest if I send you back to him, as soon as you are warm again. I do not like the look of the sky."

"Only look how big these kittens have got," Jane exclaimed as she knelt by their basket. "Why they are almost cats! What a fine and kind gift they were, d'you not think?"

"Indeed," Marianne laughed, looking down at the well-rounded kittens. "This house was suffering from a desperate overabundance of cream, from which the dear creatures have contrived to save us!"

As Jane stroked the kittens and scratched them under their chins, they purred loudly and stretched. Then she caught Marianne's eye again. "The doctor is very kind, d'you not think?"

"Of course," Marianne returned. "There can be no denying that."

Jane glanced at Becky, then took Marianne by the hand and looked up at her with big eyes. "The doctor is handsome, too, d'you not think?"

Marianne was rather taken aback by this question, which had been asked in tones of the utmost seriousness. "I do," she answered with equal gravity.

"What I think is," Jane went on implacably, "is that the doctor is the kindest, most handsomest man there ever was." She waited for a response from Marianne, but, receiving none, she added with a hopeful expression, "D'you not think?"

Marianne laughed and shook her head, touched at the child's transparent machinations. She wondered briefly if it were at all possible that such an inquisition was prompted in some way by Venables's own curiosity; the notion was dismissed almost at once, however, as being unconscionably whimsical.

"And how," she asked lightly, "am I to answer that, I would like to know? I have no means of judging him against all the men that ever were!"

Jane knit her brow. " 'Tis true enough," she allowed. Then Becky whispered in her ear, and Jane's bright eyes lit with an expression which could only be described as calculating. "But of all the men *you've* ever known," she said triumphantly, "how fares the doctor there?"

Marianne hid her smile. "Very well, if you must know. Very well indeed."

"That is *not*," Jane told her sternly, "how you would say it in a tale, now is it?"

Marianne shook her head. "But this is not a tale," she reminded them. "But come, the two of you, and sit by me, and I shall tell you a brief fairy story. When I have done, however, I must send you back home."

She poured them each a cup of tea and added plenty of cream and sugar, just as they liked it, and gathered them on either side of her. "There was once a princess," she began, "who lived under a cruel enchantment. She was full of things she wished to say, but alas, an unkind fairy had stolen her voice. She could neither speak nor sing, and all the thoughts of her heart and mind must be expressed in her eyes or gestures."

"Like Becky does?" Jane whispered.

Marianne gave them each a little hug. "But Becky *can* speak when she's a mind to," she amended. "She simply does not drop her pearls of wisdom harum-scarum."

" 'Tis so," Jane agreed.

Becky gave a little sigh and snuggled closer. Marianne looked down at their auburn curls and felt her heart begin to fill. This was exactly how she needed to spend her day. "The princess," she went on, "wanted nothing more than to tell what was in her heart, but all her lovely thoughts were kept prisoner inside of her, like little caged birds who had forgotten how to sing—"

"Someone's coming," Jane interrupted her, tugging at her sleeve.

Marianne looked up to see a figure enter her

garden and approach the French doors. It was not the doctor, she knew at once. Something about him looked familiar, however, something that sent a chill to her very core, like the return of a childhood nightmare.

A moment later, Sir Frederick Stratford stepped into the room.

Sixteen

Sir Frederick Stratford! Marianne's head whirled in a storm of disbelief. This could not, could *not* be. All of her precious security, all of her joy, the very notion of who she was, evaporated about her as soon as she recognized him.

Stratford smiled slowly, triumph in his eyes. "Hello, Marianne. You will pardon me, I am sure, for disturbing this pretty little domestic scene," he said as he calmly drew off his greatcoat and flung it over a chair. "I had an odd notion, however, that, were I announced, you might try to evade me. Under normal circumstances, I might even enjoy the chase, but unfortunately time does not permit me the luxury of such a tantalizing pursuit."

As if sensing her alarm, Jane and Becky clutched at Marianne's arms, and their small gesture of vulnerability helped her to gather herself and marshal her senses.

"Go, children," she whispered to them in an urgent undertone. "You must go at once."

"What? No introductions? Tut, my dear. It is not like you to be so discourteous." Stratford came toward them and studied the children for a moment, a look of cold calculation lighting his eyes. "So, Marianne, it seems you have been holding out on us all. And whose pretty little by-blows are these, pray tell?"

The sound of the clock on the mantelpiece was deafening in the grim silence that followed. With growing alarm, Marianne could feel the little girls stiffen next to her at his scrutiny; she tried surreptitiously to prod them forward, to make them leave, but they clung to her all the tighter.

"Not Cheswick's, of course," he mused, "but who came before him? Can they be Clivedon's, I wonder?"

She regarded him with stony silence, her sensibilities barely registering this insult, but her mind raced. What was she to do? Could it possibly matter now?

When she spoke at last, the calmness of her own voice surprised her. "Pray, Stratford, allow me to send the children away. We cannot converse thus."

He laughed. "Ever the expedient one, my Marianne. By all means, you may send the brats to Hades for aught I care. They do not concern me."

Gently, she pushed them away from her. "Do as I say," she told them. The pair regarded her rebelliously, their eyes flashing dangerously at the intruder. "Do not worry," she said, attempting lightness. "I am sure it is almost time for your dinner in any case."

Reluctantly, the girls slid from the sofa, and,

casting many a backward look, at last left the room. When the door had closed behind them, Stratford came and sat beside Marianne. "How exceedingly inconvenient it is," he said, curling his lip in disgust, "to discover you are still so exceedingly *enceinte*, Marianne. My calculations were in error, I am afraid."

"I do not know how you found me," she cried, her composure deserting her, "nor what your design is in coming here, but I beg you will go away at once."

"Little Marianne." He shook his head. "You do not know what my design is, eh? I assure you, dissembling will do you no good, my dear. I mean, you must know, to take you away and make some use of you. Your fine charade is done here. We shall set out at first light tomorrow, if the weather clears."

In such a hurry, she thought quickly. Stratford must be truly under the hatches, or worse, to take to flight. She might, perhaps, use his distress to her benefit. If only he could be got rid of quickly, before he was able to do real harm.

"I assure you," she said smoothly, "even had I the desire to go with you— which you must know I have not— I am in no condition to travel. The child will arrive any day now— "

"Women have borne children on the road before this," he interrupted coldly, "and my need cannot be easily fulfilled without you."

"I care nothing for your needs!" she spat at him.

"You made that quite clear to me in London,"

he returned with a chilling smile. "Nevertheless, you will come with me. I have a notion that your reappearance in London will prompt an indispensable infusion of capital to my poor purse."

Marianne gasped. "You cannot mean blackmail!"

"What an ugly word," he said. "Let us say instead that, for a small price, I will find it convenient to spare our poor friend Cheswick an embarrassment which might prove deleterious to his marriage. And such a thing is so much easier to achieve when incontrovertible evidence is present in the flesh, shall we say? No," he concluded, "I am afraid there is nothing for it but for you to return to the city with me. You have already inconvenienced me sufficiently."

Marianne felt her fingers curl into fists as rage as the realization of his perfidy overcame her. "I will not be a party to this wickedness," she whispered. "You cannot force me."

His smile of satisfaction grew wider. "Ah, but I can. I do not at all like to be unpleasant," he went on, "but you do not seem to collect the *difficulties* that will undoubtedly accompany your refusal." He paused a moment, watching her. "Your sister, for instance. It would very likely discomfit her mightily were tales of your adventures— not to mention all these children— to reach the ears of certain parties. She is seen everywhere, and her lord as well. What might her feelings be, were society reminded who and what her sister is?"

Hatred unlike any she had before experienced

seethed through her. How could anyone be so wicked? It was as if he had no soul.

"And then there is the matter of this amusing masquerade you have perpetrated here," he continued silkily. "I think I could not depart this neighborhood without first informing the good parson of your true character— yes, I took the trouble to make his acquaintance and that of his wife today. I am afraid you have little choice, my dear. You may refuse to come with me, but by all counts, you cannot remain here."

Marianne looked at Stratford narrowly. There was more to this business than he was telling. If blackmail came so easily to him, she was certain he must have hoarded many secrets over the years. It was well known, too, that Cheswick's fortune was controlled by his wife's family. Could it be that his real aim was to ruin two lives?

He threw back his head and laughed. "Such hatred on your pretty face is unbecoming, Marianne. It is, of course, your fault we have come to this. I believe I told you some time ago that I wanted you. I have a deplorable penchant, you know, for getting my way— by foul means or fair. Or, if I cannot, to make my displeasure felt. You should have obliged me before, in London, and we could have avoided all this regrettable unpleasantness."

Marianne felt her heart go numb with increased anger and deadening shock. She knew in that moment that she was capable of murder, had she a weapon or the strength. But she had neither at the moment. She must think. She must take deep breaths and concentrate. Slowly, a stiletto of pain worked its way up her back. Gritting her teeth against it, she schooled her countenance and forced herself to smile.

"As for the manner in which you have chosen to work your will," she began, "I will say nothing. I scarcely think you can be shamed by my reading you a scold."

"Not in the least," he returned with a bow. He took out his snuffbox and applied a pinch with insufferable composure.

"It seems you leave me little choice, but to go with you," she said quietly, "as I am sure you must know."

He sneezed delicately into a handkerchief, and smiled again. "You are very wise, my dear."

"Perhaps," she allowed. "But you may yourself be very foolish." She allowed him a moment to take this in. The pain raced up her back again, more intensely this time. She felt the perspiration break out on her forehead, but willed herself to go on. "It is unwise," she continued raggedly, "to make an enemy of someone who has nothing to lose."

His eyes narrowed. "What do you mean?"

"I mean that you may choose to destroy the life I have built here. But all actions have their consequences."

She smiled inwardly to see his eyes grow wary. "I shall warn you but once: when you least expect it, I shall find the means to kill you. You will never again be safe to eat or sleep or turn your back on me. I will be avenged eventually, and you will be very, very sorry."

She had not known herself what she meant to say until the words formed on her tongue. Having said them, she felt the shock doubly, both by hearing them in her heart and seeing her adversary pale in response to them. Stratford's countenance was washed with loathing. Suddenly, it was clear to her: he truly hated her. She could think of no reason, but there was no escaping the conclusion that it had never been her body he truly wished, but dominion over her. He did not so much want *her*, as he wanted to see her broken to his will.

He rose from his seat slowly, like a snake uncoiling, and loomed over her. Violence shone in his eyes. She shrank before his rage, clasping her arms protectively about her.

Venables strode along the winding path, the boys trailing behind him. He gathered his greatcoat tightly around him. The storm that had been threatening all afternoon was beginning to bear down, and now it was discovered that Jane and Becky were missing. They were not in the house or the barn; it stood to reason they were at their usual haunt, Rosewood Cottage.

He had been hoping to pay a call there all day, but two emergencies had arisen in the afternoon, keeping him occupied until he judged it too late for such an endeavor. Even though he suspected that the girls' disappearance was linked to their attempts at matchmaking, he was not in the least loath to go in search of them— only the threat of the storm gave him any misgiving at their action. In any case, he would have the pleasure of looking in on Marianne, even if it meant coming home sodden and cold.

Against the horizon, a flash of lightning lit the sky. The thunder followed almost immediately, prompting him to quicken his step.

"Charlie! George!" he called over his shoulder. "Try to keep pace with me, or I shall be sorry I brought you along!"

Hurriedly, they came up beside him. As they rounded a bend, they came almost immediately upon the huddled forms of Jane and Becky, looking back over their shoulders in the direction of Rosewood Cottage.

"Here you are!" Venables called. When they turned to him, he could see that Jane's face was pale and wide-eyed, while tears coursed down Becky's cheeks.

"What is this?" he asked, kneeling beside them.

"Please, we didna like to go from her, doctor," Jane said, her small voice wavering. "Only she commanded us to and, oh, we are so feared for her."

Venables felt his heart grow still. "Why? What do you mean?"

"It is a man," Jane cried.

Becky tugged at his sleeve. "A man who is wicked," she whispered.

Seventeen

Venables broke into a run, leaving the children to trail behind him. As he raced toward the cottage, the sky suddenly opened, and thick slanting sheets of rain began to pour down on him. He did not know what he might find, but his heart had frozen at the recognition of fear in Jane's and Becky's faces. This was no mere machination to place him at the widow's door.

The wind tore at him furiously as he reached the door. He flung it open and all but threw himself in. Annie greeted him with shocked surprise.

"Why, Doctor Venables! What? Out in this storm? Whatever are you about?"

"Where is Mrs. Glencoe?" he gasped.

"Why, she is in the drawing room, I suppose—"

"Take your shawl," he interrupted. "The children are just down the lane. Take them to Mrs. Maiden as fast as you may."

He did not wait for an answer, but made his way quickly to the drawing room. From inside, he now heard the sound of furniture falling and Marianne's low cry. Near blind with apprehension, he jerked the door open with such force it nearly left its hinges. Before him he saw Marianne, trying desperately to protect herself from an assailant.

Her face already bore the mark of a cuff, and the man was raising his hand yet again. Venables catapulted through the door, took the cur by the shoulders, and threw him bodily to the floor.

Marianne stared in horror at the scene before her. Stunned, Stratford moaned as he attempted to recover from Venables's sudden assault. When he looked up, his face registered a look of astonished incredulity as he took in the sight of the doctor looming over him.

"I see you have found another protector, Marianne," he managed at last, his eyes dark with rage. He glanced again at Venables. "I wonder what she has told you?"

Marianne stiffened.

"Not another word," Venables said, "or you will know what it is to be silenced with your own teeth." Marianne was shocked at the violence in his voice. It was as if a sudden unsuspected aspect of his soul had been bared by the brutality of the scene he had interrupted, and a dragon had emerged.

Keeping a watchful eye on Stratford, Venables asked, "Are you much hurt, Mrs. Glencoe?"

"Is that what you are calling yourself these days, Marianne?" Stratford muttered insinuatingly. "A widow, I take it. How I should like to have been able to see you through what I am certain must have been an exceedingly dark period of mourning."

Venables jerked forward, but Marianne stayed him. "Please," she whispered, her voice breaking. "Please, no more."

Stratford still had not moved from the floor, but his eyes now glittered treacherously. "She is not worth it, you know," he said. "Were I you, I should not trouble myself with the slut— or her bastard."

Stratford's words assailed Marianne with the shock of yet another blow, and, simultaneously, a band of agonizing pain seized her.

"No!" she gasped weakly, but Venables had already lunged at Stratford. The doctor's face was white, as he hauled the man to his feet and dragged him through the door. She was in too much agony to protest further, but she could hear the front door open, and Stratford's curse become one with the howl of the storm.

She concentrated on her pain, glad in one sense of a way to remove herself from the worse agony of the scene she had just witnessed. Life mirrored nature. The storm which had just broken in her consciousness threatened to be far more destructive than the one which raged just beyond her window.

In what seemed a mere moment, Venables was at her side again, his presence now not in the least comforting. Stratford's words could not have left any doubt in the doctor's mind of who and what she was. If only she could persuade him to go away, that she might be left alone with her pain and disgrace.

He settled his arm gently about her. "Do not

worry— I have sent the blackguard into the night with a fair expectation of what he might receive were he to return. Are you injured?" he whispered.

The pain had subsided again. She shook her head, as the tears began to slide down her face. Stratford's words echoed in her mind. Slut. Bastard. That Venables should have heard him outweighed the torment of physical pain. It was as if she had been ruined again.

Still, he held her, and his voice was gentle. She searched her mind for words that would explain everything, would make the shame go away, but none would form. She was now weeping uncontrollably, and only her shuddering conveyed the least whisper of what she wished to convey.

Venables stroked her hair and made soothing noises, as if she were a child who had taken some hurt. "My Marianne," he whispered.

Her heart was torn asunder by his tenderness, his goodness. Surely he must have heard, must have understood the import of Stratford's vicious revelation. But perhaps goodness could not comprehend evil. Perhaps he simply did not believe it of her.

All at once, she was racked with another series of pains, and she doubled over, trying desperately not to cry out.

"Dear God!" Venables cried. "How long has this been going on?"

She shook her head. She had no clear idea how much time had passed.

"Do not be afraid," he said gently. "The shock has prompted a premature labor. Let me know when the pain subsides, and I shall carry you up to your chamber."

She was torn between the desire to send him away and the fear for the child she carried, when suddenly she remembered. "What about the girls?" she whispered.

"It is all right," he said, with an attempt to reassure her. "I have sent Annie after them, and the boys are with them now."

"But what if he should come across them?" she gasped. "Stratford is mad and evil— Annie could do nothing. Go to them, please," she begged. "There is already too much I cannot forgive myself . . ."

He frowned in consternation, clearly at odds with himself. "I cannot leave you like this."

"You must," she urged. "I shall manage . . . Ring— Mrs. Bridges will hear and come to me."

"All right," he acquiesced, "but do not think I shall leave it to chance. I shall fetch the woman to you before I depart."

"Just hurry," she gasped. "Hurry."

After he had disposed Marianne to her servant's care, Venables once more faced the storm. The light was by now exceedingly dim; only a few vague shapes stood out in the torrential rain. He wished to God he had a horse, saddled and ready, for he had grave misgivings about leaving Marianne alone. First pregnancies were dangerous, especially when labor was premature. He was afoot, however, and now he traced the path, making the best speed he could through the tempest.

He could hear nothing but the storm, could feel nothing but fear, rage, and the penetrating rain. There was no sign of the person Marianne had called Stratford. He was not surprised: only a coward would have attacked a woman. Doubtless he had ridden away to the cesspool from which he had sprung.

When he reached the crossroads, Venables paused for a moment, wiping the rain from his eyes. At first he saw nothing. Then the lightning flashed, illuminating the landscape. In that brief instant he perceived a rider in the distance, rearing on his mount before the scattering figures of the children and Annie. Then all was black again.

The chill hand of the past gripped his heart: children about to be ridden down. And Annie. Poor crippled Annie. Driven by instinct, he darted forward to put himself before the rider. Thunder cracked like the whip of an angry god. He could hear now the horse's terrified screech mingled with the cries of the children, and it spurred him on.

In a brief flash he saw how he might seize the reins, but the next dark instant blinded him once more and his grip closed on nothing. Small hands snatched at his coat and pulled him away from his object. Thunder, then lightning again revealed the rearing horse mad with fright. At the next clap, it bolted to the west, Stratford bending low to grip its mane.

He heard his name cried out, as if from a host of small voices.

"Dr. Venables!" Annie cried. "I am so sorry," she moaned. "I mistook the way in the storm and—"

"We must gather the children and go back to Rosewood," he interrupted. He reached down and could feel the curly heads of Jane and Becky at his knee. "Charlie! George!" he shouted.

"Over here!" He did not know which of the boys had called to him, but he ran in the direction whence the voice had come. In a moment he reached them, and a flicker from the sky revealed Charlie bent down over his brother's form.

"It is George," he cried, "and he does not move."

Venables knelt at the child's side, sought his neck, and gently tested for a pulse. It was there, strong but somewhat erratic. He heaved a sigh of relief.

"It hurts," he heard the child gasp.

"Where?"

"My chest— it was the horse, I think. Will I die?"

"Hush. Of course not."

"That is well," George sighed. "I should not at all like to be an angel in heaven."

Venables scooped him up in his arms. "Annie," he called over his shoulder. "Are you equal to fetching Maggie?"

"Why yes, but why— ?"

"Mrs. Glencoe has gone into labor. Go back to Rosewood first and fetch a lantern, for it will be fully dark ere long. I shall see to George and the others."

"Yes, doctor," she said faintly.

"You are not afraid, I hope?"

She gave a brave little laugh. "I am sore afraid, but there's naught else to be done, is there?"

"Take Charlie along with you. It will take his mind off his brother to have some errand. Run along now. You are a good girl, Annie."

Eighteen

In those brief periods between the racking pains, Marianne lost herself to wretched speculation. What was to become of her and her child now? She could not stay where her secret must soon be known, for though Venables seemed confident he had put Stratford to flight, she feared he might still contrive to make good his threat to reveal her secret to the Wallers. The notion of those good people coming to know what she had been sent a tremor of humiliation through her.

And the doctor, what of him? That was worst of all, for she recognized that, through him, she had achieved what she had scarcely dreamed of hoping for: the respect of a decent man. Now that all hope was gone, she also recognized with a sinking heart that she had come to love him dearly. She would never have dreamed of revealing her feelings, but they might have remained a small treasure in the corner of her heart. A keepsake of what might have been. That was all over. She must, she knew, tell him of her past, explain the scene he had interrupted.

Regardless of any other consideration, though,

her child was coming. What was to become of it? It was one thing to envision fleeing once again to shield them both from censure, but how that might be accomplished and whence they might escape was another thing altogether. The greater part of the monies she had accumulated had been spent on Rosewood Cottage, and she knew she was not likely to find another buyer for it any time soon. Without funds, she would soon have no other recourse than to return to her former way of life, and that was not to be thought of.

Turning restlessly in her bed, she almost wished that this brief respite from pain might be over, for it at least disallowed the invasion of such rambling, useless thoughts. Time brought her nothing but wretched confusion. If only she could concentrate long enough to think clearly what might be done to ameliorate the damage Stratford had done, if not for her own sake, then for the babe's.

In the dim light, she saw that Old Maggie bent over her now, smoothing a stray hair off her forehead.

"I have brought you some valerian tea," she said. "You must drink it right down all at once, for I have made it so strong it is quite bitter. It will help you to relax, though. A long night it will be, and you will have need of all your strength."

Marianne took the cup from her and did as the older woman said. A bitter cup, she thought abstractedly. What else should it be?

"Believe me that all shall be well, mistress,"

Maggie said kindly. "I do not always see the future, but when I do, I do not see amiss. Close your eyes for a bit, and listen to the rain. 'Tis a healing sound. And I am at your side."

When Dr. Venables was at last able to leave George's side, he found the night had calmed somewhat. The wind still blew, but without the ferocity which had earlier accompanied it, and the rain now fell gently upon the land. The boy, he had been relieved to find, had not been badly hurt. The horse's hooves had thankfully missed his head, and glanced his shoulder and chest instead. By some providence, nothing was broken, but he was in a good deal of pain. Venables had dressed the lad's wounds and dosed him with laudanum, then saddled his horse and returned once again the way he had come.

He knew that Marianne was in good hands with Maggie. Whatever their differences, he knew she was a skilled midwife in whom he might place his confidence. Still, he was plagued with visions of Marianne at the hands of that villain, and wretched with worry lest the shock she had sustained might have some unsuspected deleterious effect on her system. The mind and the body, he knew, were linked in ways medicine had yet to discover.

Of the assailant's words, he had thought little until now, on this solitary ride through the night. One thought tumbled over the other, defying logical order. Whence came this demon, and how had one as gentle as Marianne become entangled with such a brute? And if the words the man had spoken of her were the truth, if they were not some vile fabrication . . . ?

Venables shook himself. The past, his own and hers, did not figure, he told himself staunchly. Words, mere words. If Marianne wished to speak of it, she might do so, but he would not importune her with questions. He had no right.

Such a resolution was difficult, nay impossible, to keep to, however. As he steered his mount along the dark pathways, various questions and explanations presented themselves. What he could not rationalize away was the feeling that, regardless of what the truth of the matter might be, his heart was still engaged. It made no odds. It was clear she required love and protection. If she would accept his, he might be a happy man.

As he approached the cottage, he heard the patter of footsteps as Charlie ran up to him from the doorway where he had been keeping watch. "Is George dead?" he asked falteringly.

"Not in the least," the doctor said, laying a hand on the child's shoulder. "Bruised and battered, but still among the living. When I left him, he was asking for biscuits!"

In the light from the doorway, he could see that the boy's eyes were sparkling with tears. Sniffling a bit, he wiped these away with his sleeve and summoned a smile, saying, "God's a knowin' fellow and sees what's best, for what George said was right— he would make a very bad angel."

Venables laughed softly as he entered the vestibule. "So he would," he agreed. "Have you found a place to sleep?"

The boy nodded. "Mrs. Bridges made me snug by the fire here, but I could not sleep 'til you were come." He yawned hugely then, shifting from one foot to another.

"Off to bed then," Venables said.

The child nodded and made as if to do so, then turned and said, "You see. It is just as we thought. Best to marry Mrs. Glencoe, and you and us boys shall protect her better. 'Tis no good for her to be alone."

Words of wisdom, Venables thought as he ascended the staircase. Just as he reached Marianne's chamber, however, he encountered Maggie coming out of it.

She raised a finger to her lips. "Hush," she said. "She has only been able to close her eyes these last minutes. I gave her a stout cup of valerian tea, which I think has settled her somewhat. The pains have subsided for the nonce, but unless I am far afield, we shall see the child before morning. But come, let us go down to the kitchen and have a sup of tea. I have left the mistress in Mrs. Bridges's good care. She will call to us, if we are needed."

He placed a hand on the door, loath to go away without having at least looked in on the lady. Maggie nodded to him, and he went in. Marianne lay still for the moment, her dark hair spread out on the pillows like a cloud. Mrs.

Bridges sat in a chair at her side, busying herself with a length of drab-colored knitting.

He stood quietly a moment, glad at least to see that Marianne had been granted a respite, however brief it might prove to be, from the torments she had lately suffered. The physical pain would be gone eventually, but her wounded spirit, he knew, would take far longer in healing.

Though he was already weary, he did not at all wish to leave her. "Go ahead, Maggie," he said. "I shall join you presently."

He sent Mrs. Bridges off to her bed, and took the chair at the bedside. A bruise was beginning to darken Marianne's cheek, and he cursed beneath his breath. A doctor should not, he knew, indulge in violent thoughts, but he would have given all to have wrung the neck of the villain who had dared to injure his love. As he pulled his chair closer, he saw Marianne's eyelids flutter, then open. As she recognized him, she turned away her head.

"Go away," she whispered. "You are far too good. You need not stay, now you know the worst of me."

"The worst I know of you," he said softly, taking her hand in his, "is that you are too full of love."

She shook her head and pulled her hand away. "I have threatened a man with murder today. And before that, I have sinned, sinned past count."

"Hush. You know nothing of sin. If you have threatened that man—no matter. No one condemns the shepherd for defending his flock against the wolf. I do not know what he held up to you, but—"

"I must tell you," she said.

"No," he said firmly. She had had a great deal too many shocks for one day. Doubtless, if he allowed her to speak, the morning would bring regret.

She gripped his sleeve. "You already know or have guessed part. I would rather you knew the whole."

"I must beg of you, Mrs. Glencoe . . ." he pleaded.

She shook her head. "That is not my name." She looked beseechingly at him. "Please, please, you must listen to me."

He nodded, and she seemed to relax somewhat. Perhaps it was best, after all, if the telling would help to ease her mind.

In the darkened room, her words tumbled over each other: the story of a young girl named Marianne Gardiner entering the jaded world of the *ton,* full of hope and romance. She told him of her flirtation with the Marquis de la Roche, his attentions and flattery, and finally his betrayal.

"I knew I should not have gone to him," she whispered. "But I was headstrong, certain I knew what was best, certain my life would fall into the perfect lines of a fairy tale. I slipped away and met him in a park, thinking he might perhaps try to kiss me, but no worse. I even cherished a hope he might offer for me— not because I fancied myself in love. It merely would have suited my pride to count such a distinguished gentleman among my conquests.

"When I reached the park, I found he had his carriage waiting. I protested, but he laughed at me and coaxed me inside— and took me to his house. His servants had been sent away for the afternoon, he told me, so I need not worry that my visit there would be reported. He seemed very kind, at first, merely interested in showing me his collections— music boxes, exotic bibelots, such things as would appeal to a young girl's fancy."

She was silent for a moment then, and Venables took her hand. She barely returned the pressure of his fingers.

"Before I knew it," she went on wearily, "we had found ourselves in an empty chamber. That is when he— he forced me to his will." She swallowed hard and shut her eyes. "I was so stupid, so horribly stupid. How could I not have seen— "

Venables chafed her hand between his. "Hush, my love," he said. He felt his jaws tighten as he saw the tears shining on her eyelashes. He felt an anger, greater even than he had felt for Stratford, rise up in him. He had not known de la Roche, but had certainly heard of him in his younger days. The man had, in fact, been something of a hero to that debauched set to which he had himself once belonged. He shuddered now to think of it.

"When he had done with me," Marianne continued in a hollow voice, "he had his carriage drop me just beyond my own home. I was confused and distraught—I did not keep my secret long. My mother has sharp eyes and soon knew something was amiss. My parents were not prepared to hear my revelations with . . . equanimity, and I was still too headstrong to long bear what I viewed as their tyranny and rancor. They kept me locked away in my room until they could discover whether or not I was increasing— thank God I was not!

"One night, I ran away. In a matter of days, I was back with the marquis. There was no other place to go. He kept me for a year or so, then I formed other liaisons. I made my way in the world as only a woman in my fallen state could. Through sin."

As he listened to Marianne's story, he recognized it. He had heard it before, as had everyone in the *ton*. That the subject of it should prove to be one so gentle and good, that she should have been sinned against by all and sundry, tore his heart. No, he thought— regardless of self-condemnation, she knew nothing of sin. He stroked her hand and her hair, as the candle guttered in its holder. He knew he would tell her his story when the time was right. It would do nothing to raise him in her opinion, but at least then, she would know what sin was.

When Marianne slept at last, spent by the turmoil of her confession, he left her again to Mrs. Bridges's care, then stepped out into the corridor and followed it down the stairs to the kitchen. The fire still glowed, and a kettle sat warming at the hearthside. In the shadows, he could see Maggie, staring into the embers.

"I will brew us a tisane, doctor," Maggie said, as he entered. A linen bag hung from her waist, and he watched as she procured from this several small bags he supposed to contain herbs. When she had stirred them into an earthenware pot, she turned to him and indicated a low bench by the fireside. "Come join me here," she said.

He did as she suggested, waiting quietly until the tea had brewed. At last, she poured out a mug of fragrant, steaming liquid and held it out to him. He took it from her and breathed deep. Almost at once, he felt soothed and refreshed. She was a redoubtable woman, this Maggie.

"I am glad you are here for this birth," he told her. "I have wanted to see you at work for some time. Your reputation borders on mythic, you know."

She shrugged away the compliment. "Time will tell. I do not think this will prove the most difficult I have seen, as first births go."

"I am by no means convinced of that," he said ruefully. "Mrs. Glencoe has undergone a shock this afternoon. I am glad there was . . ."

"Aye. It is another woman she is in need of this night. Men have not been good to her, you see."

He looked at her sharply. Her eyes sparkled back at him, as if she read his thoughts.

"She's told me nothing in words. I have only read what is in her face, and in her heart. You have done the same, have you not? The pain of the past is written there clear enough for those who will see."

True, he had perused that mysterious text since he had first met the lady, but to little avail. This night's revelation only made the matter more thorny.

"I am not certain," he said slowly, "what I have read there."

In the darkness, her low chuckle sounded like a dry leaf crumbling. "You need not hold back with me, doctor. It is the tradition of healers, you know, that they may speak freely with one another. Or are you still so much of that other world that your lips will not let 'scape an honest word?"

What she implied was true. Venables had done what he could to exorcise the demons of his life in the *ton,* but it was still a part of him in the form of reticence and closely guarded secrets. For all he had tried to be free of the past, her words brought him reeling back. Outside, the wind howled mournfully. "What would you know of that world?" he asked.

"More than enough to see it is bounded by hypocrisy on the one side, and fear on the other," she returned tartly.

"Hypocrisy, yes. There can be no denying that," he agreed. "But fear? How do you mean?"

"What we all fear: that we are human." She stared into the fire for a long moment. "The quality— they act as if true feelings were not for such as they," she went on, "as if this life were but a game to outdance death. They blind themselves to the truth: their sparkles and fine ways are nothing. In the end, we all suffer the same fate, countess or scullery maid.

"Now, you and Mrs. Glencoe are different, though you've sprung from that world," she said with a sharp glance at him. "The shadow of the past is still upon you, but you've come through hell, the both of you, and see sometimes with clearer eyes."

"Only sometimes?" he asked.

"Aye," she nodded. "Neither one of you can see what's written plainly before you, what even little children can see."

He remained silent, hoping she would say more. Perhaps this strange woman knew as well as he what was written in his heart and Marianne's, but he sensed that direct questions would not serve him here. Maggie seemed content to let the silence hang between them for the moment, though she did not take her eyes from him. He busied himself building up the fire, for the room had grown quite chill.

When he had addressed this task, he found himself anxious for further conversation, and unnerved by what had been left unsaid. "You criticize my reticence," he said quietly, "yet you will do no more than talk in riddles. Tell me what more you know, Maggie, if it is honesty you value."

"Aye, I value it well enough," she said. "You

have caught me out— not many do. As for riddles, that is the shape my knowledge comes in.
I do not always know what it means myself, and
must often guess." She looked up from the fire
and caught his eye. "Very well. I do not have
leave to tell you all, but I will say what I may.

"I look at your face and the mistress's, and I
see you've traveled much the same path, and
ended at the same spot: regret. Aye, but there's
the need for forgiveness, too, more for yourself
than others. Is that a riddle now, or do you think
I speak more plain?"

Venables felt his heart start at these words.
True, she did not speak in terms a stranger
would have been able to interpret; as for their
application to his and Marianne's various histo-
ries, her words held true. Still, he frowned in
consternation, feeling as if he knew both more
and less than he had before.

He heard just then the sound of Mrs.
Bridges's step in the passage. "Come quick," she
called to them. " 'Tis the mistress in a mortal
bad way. She be thrashing about and talking
wild."

Nineteen

Venables tore up the stairs, while Maggie followed at a less hurried pace. When he gained the chamber he sought, he was greeted with the sight of Marianne thrashing wildly, as if caught in the throes of a nightmare.

"I do not know what's come over her," Mrs. Bridges said in apprehension. "She was sleeping peacefully enough, then woke with a start, saying it was all to pieces here, and she must fly."

Joining them, Maggie took the lady's arm and, leading her away, said, "Pay it no heed, Mrs. Bridges. I have seen it thus more than once. It is the pain and the fright with these first children. Do go to bed and rest yourself now. I shall call, if you are needed."

When they were left alone, Maggie went on, " 'Tis better if we are left in peace to our work. Sally Bridges is no gossip, but still 'tis best if the mistress has her privacy. Households run better where there's nothing to repeat."

Venables nodded, and crossed to the bed to take stock of the situation. As he approached, Marianne turned her head away from him, tears still glistening on her lashes. He knelt and caressed her forehead.

"I am being punished for my folly and sin," she whispered. "I thought I could outwit fate. I thought I could be happy."

"Poor soul," Maggie whispered.

"Mrs. Glencoe sustained a nasty shock this afternoon," he explained quietly as he chafed Marianne's wrist. "Sometimes the full effects of such shocks are not immediately realized. It is bad enough her child is come early, but her mind seems disordered as well."

Venables was far more distraught than his calm manner indicated. To hear the despair in her voice, see the tears streaming down her face, to know the pain the night held in store for her, was overwhelming. If only he might bear some part of the burden.

Marianne moaned and reached for his arm. "You must promise me something," she murmured.

"Anything," he said softly.

"If I should die tonight— "

"No! You will not die. Do you not see? Why, Maggie and I are with you. Together we can— "

"But if I *should* die," she went on implacably, "promise you will send my baby to my sister. Promise me?"

"Yes," he said. "I promise. Now, do not fret yourself further."

"Olivia will love it as I would have done," Marianne whispered weakly, "treat it as I would have, never speak a word of reproach, for my past is not the baby's fault, you know."

"Of course not," Venables said soothingly.

"Do the sins of the mother pass to the child, do you think?"

"Of course not," he assured her. "Babies are good and sweet—like kittens. Do you not remember telling the children?"

She wrenched away from him then, caught up in pain so severe her skin seemed paler than the very sheets. Her hands clutched at the edges of the featherbed beneath her, till her knuckles showed white. A moment later she relaxed again.

"It is good for me to suffer, I think," she murmured. "Perhaps heaven will look kindly on my child."

They had a long night of it and into the dawn. By the time it was done, both Maggie and the doctor were glad to admit the benefit of the other's expertise. They were worn to a frazzle, for once labor had begun it became clear the child's position was breech. Here, Venables was doubly glad of Old Maggie's years of experience, for she undertook not only to guide the baby safely into life, but reassure him as well that all was going as well as it might. When it was done, she wrapped the baby, a healthy though small girl, and laid her beside her mother.

It was now well past dawn, and it had been some time since Marianne had spoken. Whether from exhaustion or sheer desperation of spirit mattered not; Venables was beside himself with

worry for her, relieved there was none other it
would be his task to reassure this night. He felt
for her pulse: it was faint, but steady.

"She will do well enough," Maggie said con-
fidently. "She is tired and overwrought. The best
cure for that is sleep, as I am sure you will agree.
I shall go below to prepare some strong beef tea
with plenty of marrow for her; it is quite a restorative."

When she left, Venables sank into the chair
at Marianne's side. She was breathing peacefully
now, and her forehead was no longer furrowed.
He prayed Maggie would be right in her assessment. Prayer was all he had left.

In her dream, Marianne walked in a field of
bright flowers, and all about her, little girls
danced in the sunlight, garlands in their hair.
In the sky above, white clouds scattered and
amassed, taking the shapes of lambs prancing
on a blue field. It was a paradise of sweetness,
the air alive with light. Never since childhood
had Marianne enjoyed such an overpowering
sense of serenity and well-being.

When her child was born, she thought with a
smile, this was just such a place to bring her to
play and be happy. She reached down to feel
where the babe rested beneath her heart, then
froze. She was not pregnant? What had become
of her child?

"Welcome, my Marianne."

The voice was near her, but at first she could

not see whence it came. The brightness of the air began to gather and take shape, and in a moment she found herself confronted with a lady, both grave and smiling.

"Do I know you?" Marianne asked.

The lady nodded. "We have met before, but I daresay you do not remember. Sit with me here, and we shall talk a moment."

Marianne shook her head. "But I must find my baby, you see. I cannot imagine where it has got to, for it isn't even born yet."

"Look below," the lady said.

Then it seemed as if the grass parted beneath her feet, and she looked down into her chamber at Rosewood. A dark-haired woman lay in the bed, and Dr. Venables and Old Maggie stood at her side. A baby was tucked at the woman's side, sleeping peacefully.

"You see. All is well with the child. With your daughter."

Marianne did not understand, but she nodded. "Who is the woman?" she asked.

"Do you not recognize her?"

The woman was pale, almost to death. The doctor put a hand to her throat for a moment, then said something Marianne could not hear to Maggie, who nodded and left the chamber. Then it was clear.

"She is . . . that is, it is I."

The lady nodded.

"Am I dead then?"

"No. Just resting after a long travail."

She watched as the doctor sat at the bedside

and smoothed her hair. He did not look at her
with contempt, though she remembered now
what had been revealed to him. It seemed, in
fact, that there was love in his eyes. She must be
mistaken, though. No man alive could hear what
he had and . . .

"You are not mistaken," the lady said softly.
"He loves you, and you him. It is yourselves you
do not love, and whom you must forgive. That
is the task I must send you back to perform.
The rest does not matter."

Below the scene began to fade, and with it
the airy landscape which had surrounded her.
The rest was sleep.

Marianne blinked awake. A candle flickered
at the bedside table, almost spent. In its light,
she could see Dr. Venables nodding in a chair,
a book open in his lap. He looked no more than
a tired little boy in the soft light. It was a comfort to see him there. Outside, the storm had
stilled at last, and she felt at peace. Pain was a
mere memory now.

She felt a stirring at her side, and peeped beneath the coverlet. There was her baby, curled
like a rosebud in a downy blanket. She was so
tiny! And so perfect! Her head was crowned
with wisps of dark curls. The soft line of brows
perched above her eyes. Her fingers curled into
little pink fists. Her chest rose and fell like a
leaf on the lapping edge of a pond.

Marianne smiled. *She is really mine*, she thought.

Mine to love. Mine to teach. Mine to share joy with.
She glanced at the doctor. His eyes were open
now and he, too, was smiling, though wearily. He
shut his book and set it on the table.

"How do you fare?" he whispered.

"Well," she returned, and meant it. "Is she
not perfection?"

He nodded. "She is indeed a beautiful child.
One would never know to look at the two of you
that there was ever a moment of anxiety." He
yawned and stretched for a moment. "What will
you call her?"

She did not hesitate. She had known the name
in her heart for a long time. "Felicity."

"It is a good choice." He stood and looked
down at them with the edge of a smile. "And
this was a good night's work."

The gray light of morning streamed in the
window. "What is the time?" she asked.

"Nearly ten, I should imagine. Try to go back
to sleep, if you can. Or would you like me to
send Annie or Maggie to you?"

She shook her head. "Let them rest."

Next to her little Felicity stirred and opened
her eyes. They were as blue as the summer sky.
She saw only herself there, not a hint of Cheswick.
"Is it all right if I hold her?"

The doctor laughed. "I should think it very
odd if it were not! Here, let me help you to sit
up."

He slipped his arm behind her shoulders and
piled more pillows behind her. Then he lifted
the baby into her arms. She curled into her

mother's arms as if into a comfortable nest, closed her eyes, and slept again.

"I shall leave the two of you alone for a bit," he said softly.

"Please don't!" she begged. "What if she should wake? I shall not know what to do!"

"You must do what comes naturally. Besides, I think she will sleep for some time yet. She has had a tiring time of it as well. Just hold her and let her grow accustomed to you. Talk to her, or sing if she awakens. You will do very well."

Twenty

For Marianne, the days that passed were full
of peace, and the role of motherhood sat as easily on her shoulders as sunlight on the hillside.
Felicity was a delight to her heart. Every time
Marianne looked at the child, she felt as if a gift
from heaven had fallen to her. Her tranquility
was marred only by the notion that, though
Stratford seemed to have quit the vicinity entirely, he might somehow have contrived to make
good on his threat to destroy her happiness. At
times, the anxiety was so overwhelming, she set
about packing trunks and preparing to leave,
then stopping when she realized with a sinking
heart that she had no other place to go.

When the Wallers called as soon as she was
equal to receiving them, however, she began to
hope that Stratford had indeed departed the
neighborhood without event. They had remarked on nothing other than the child's beauty
and expressed their concerns for her well-being.

The children came calling as well. The little
girls held Felicity, singing softly to her, while
the boys tried their luck at amusing the baby
with such toys as they had contrived to make for

her. As these were a carved soldier and a kite, they found little success in this endeavor and, often as not, amused themselves playing with the kittens instead.

Marianne often thought back to the dream she had had the night of Felicity's birth. Unlike other dreams, it did not fade. She could remember every detail, and recalling it summoned a lifting of spirits which helped her face the unknown future. Looking at her child, she knew that self-forgiveness had been accomplished, for who could regret pain which ended in such bliss?

Though quite tiny, Felicity seemed to thrive. She was alert and good-natured and, though Marianne recognized that untoward parental conceit must account for the notion, she was almost certain the child already recognized her own name.

The doctor had called only briefly in the weeks which ensued, and his absence tore at Marianne's heart. Neither he nor she had endeavored to mention the events that prefaced the night of Felicity's birth, but she knew the encounter with Stratford and the story of her past still hung between them. At the time, her history had seemed to prompt only Venables's sympathy, never his condemnation, yet now she wondered. Why did he suddenly have so little time for her? He was, she knew, too good a man to despise her; that was undoubtedly the reason, despite her best efforts, she had fallen in love with him.

Part of the reason, she amended, as the image of his face rose before her.

She sat one cold afternoon just before Yule, rocking her baby before the fire. The kittens, now almost cats, sprawled on the hearth, occasionally stretching, but for the most part seeming to revel in sheer laziness.

"Mrs. Glencoe?" Annie peeped in the doorway.

"Yes, Annie? What is it?"

" 'Tis Dr. Venables, wanting to know if you are at your leisure."

Marianne's heart fluttered at the mention of his name. She had almost given up hope of seeing him again, and she felt her pulse quicken at the mere mention of his name.

"Tell him to come in," she said, attempting unsuccessfully to keep the excitement from her tone.

The doctor entered a moment later, bearing a basket. He smiled warmly at her and the child, and she felt an answering smile on her own lips. His manner seemed somehow lighter than it had for some time, and reminded her of their first encounter.

"And how fare my ladies today?" he asked brightly.

Marianne laughed. "That depends on what is in the basket," she said. "If you have brought me a family of orphaned hedgehogs to mother, I vow I shall send you back out into the cold."

He uncovered the basket and set it at her side. "Jane and Becky have sent you some greens for

Yule. They are very sparse in these parts," he went on, "not perhaps what you are used to."

"They are lovely," she smiled as she breathed in their heady fragrance, "and all the more so when I think how the dears must have worked to find them."

Venables paused for a moment, before saying, "I bring you news as well."

These words were spoken with a gravity which alerted her at once. She ceased rocking and looked at him, her heart pounding with sudden trepidation.

His eyes searched her face. "I do not know," he said hesitantly, "whether its import will occasion relief or distress. But it is something I cannot in good conscience keep from you."

In her arms, Felicity stretched and yawned, oblivious to the tension which hung in the air. Marianne rose and set the baby in her cradle. "Whatever it is, I must hear it," she said quietly. She turned to face Venables and folded her hands before her. "Rest assured, there is little to which I am now unequal."

She seated herself once again and waited, images of doom crowding her head.

"I must tell you," he began, "how reluctant I am to bring this matter to your attention, for it will put you in mind of events I am sure you had far rather forget."

Marianne felt her heart grow chill. So her fears were justified. It was all over for her.

"The gentleman who lately caused you such distress—"

"Stratford," she whispered. "Go on."

"I do not know what he was to you," Venables said wretchedly, "but you must know the worst: he is dead."

Dead. Stratford was dead. Marianne sank back in her chair, the tension of the past weeks suddenly drained from her. Though relieved beyond measure, she found herself speechless, and could but stare.

"I should have known of the event sooner," Venables went on, "but it was an odd circumstance, you see. The day after the storm, a farmer found Stratford's horse wandering loose. Rather than reporting the incident to the magistrate, he accepted it as his good fortune, and said nothing of the matter. Stratford's body was found only this morning, at the bottom of the cliffs by the sea. We can only conjecture that he was thrown there and died almost immediately."

He looked to Marianne, hoping, it seemed, to detect some reaction. She felt the tears of relief form in her eyes and come spilling down her cheeks.

"My Marianne," Venables murmured sadly, kneeling by her side. "Forgive my clumsiness. I had not thought . . ."

She shook her head and tried to smile. "It is not that," she said through her tears. "You are not to think . . . It is just I am overcome to finally know . . . Thank God, he is gone!"

Venables reached up to touch her face. "I wish you will say no more," he said. "I assure you, what I have heard in this matter thus far, is entirely forgot. I wish you will put it from your mind."

She looked down at him, and felt the love stream forth. If he would have it that way, she felt not the least desire to protest. What was it Maggie had said? *Let the dead past bury its dead.* She was right. Marianne might at last turn her back on the dead past and, if she could, think no more on it.

"But I wish to tell you something of my own past," he went on, "for I think it may help you to sort the oddly tangled threads of fate, to show that you know nothing at all of sin." He allowed his words to drift into silence.

He stood and paced distractedly a few moments, then stopped, and faced her. "There stands before you," he said, "one who has in his life done great harm. Irreparable, so I once thought."

"Hush," she said softly. "You need not—"

"But I must. I have never told this story before, but I beg you will listen to me. Surely *you* will understand my need to tell it."

His gaze and manner were so full of earnest entreaty, she swallowed hard and nodded.

"You will have guessed," he began, "that my origins are far from this tranquil countryside. My father was a baron, and my mother the daughter of an earl. As an only child, I was indulged past all endurance. Whatever I wanted, I had. Whatever I did was praised out of all reason. I was raised, in short, to believe that the sun rose and set for my convenience.

"Not surprisingly, I grew up quite wild. Those tendencies of youth which are repressed in young women were fostered, even encouraged, in men. When I came on the town, a more dissolute excuse for a man could not have been found. I gamed and drank and kept company with those as bad as I.

"Shortly after my first season on the town, I repaired to Ravenshead, a hunting lodge we kept in the country. I took several like-minded companions with me. We did little hunting, for the most part drank and rode wild about the countryside, worrying the cattle and making life difficult for the farmers thereabout.

"We had been late at an inn one night, playing cards and drinking rum. We should have slept away our debauch there, but instead rode recklessly through the fields as dawn was beginning to break." He shook his head. "I remember the trees crashing by as I rode, and laughing as the twigs raked at my coat. I broke through into a clearing. I was on them before I knew it."

Marianne looked at him, her eyes wide with the import of what he was telling her. He knelt by her side.

"Children," he whispered. "Little girls gone a-maying. They scattered before me, their flowers flying, but one of them fell. I could not stop my horse in time and rode her down."

He said nothing more for a moment. The silence around them reverberated with the horrible scene he had just depicted. Marianne lay a hand on his head and stroked it, as if he were a small boy.

"The child, you see, was Annie."

"Annie," she gasped. "But how— ?"

"She has never remembered anything of the incident. Her parents died the next year, and I took her into my care."

"Renounced a barony and devoted your life to medicine," she whispered.

"I have done what I could. Powers greater than I have used me for their tool. I follow the dictates of my heart, knowing it is inspired by the will of Heaven." He looked at her speakingly. "And Heaven has granted me love."

She pressed her hands to her cheeks, entirely at a loss. Of despair she knew a great deal, but of happiness almost nothing. How must she respond? He knew the worst of her; indeed they knew the worst of one another. At her side, he picked up a small leather-bound volume from the table and riffled through it.

"When first we met," he said softly, "we quoted lines from *The Tempest*. But we neglected the bard's best words." He found his place and read to her, " 'Let us not burthen our remembrances with a heaviness that's gone.' The nightmare is over for both of us. I pray you will let go the past, Marianne, and accept me as your future."

She knew that if she tried to speak, she would sink once more into tears, so full was her heart. She could picture the years ahead, full of children, their own and those who were drawn to them to be mended. Years full of laughter and

love. She raised her eyes to him and nodded.
He took her hands and drew her to him. She
came without demure. In the firelight's glow,
they held one another calmly, lovingly, with
faithful expectation of a lifetime spent thus.

*Those who looked down from above smiled in ap-
proval, as they watched the future unfold against a
dim horizon of years. They saw sisters reunite, small
cousins meet and embrace, and a hundred hearts open
like flowers in the grace these lives endowed. From
the cradle, Felicity murmured in her sleep, basking in
the golden light of forgiveness.*